NICOLA MARSH

A Trip with the Tycoon

ESCAPE
AROUND
the
WORLD

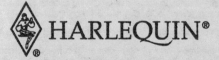

HARLEQUIN®

TORONTO • NEW YORK • LONDON
AMSTERDAM • PARIS • SYDNEY • HAMBURG
STOCKHOLM • ATHENS • TOKYO • MILAN • MADRID
PRAGUE • WARSAW • BUDAPEST • AUCKLAND

For Uncle Ian and Rayner, who kindly shared
their recent memories of the "Palace on Wheels"
as I wrote this. Thanks for the photos, the anecdotes,
the laughs—and for bringing the trip alive.

Recycling programs
for this product may
not exist in your area.

ISBN-13: 978-0-373-17611-3

A TRIP WITH THE TYCOON

First North American Publication 2009.

Copyright © 2009 by Nicola Marsh.

www.eHarlequin.com

Printed in U.S.A.

Nicola Marsh has always had a passion for writing and reading. As a youngster she devoured books when she should have been sleeping, and she later kept a diary, which could be an epic in itself! These days, when she's not enjoying life with her husband and son in her home city of Melbourne, she's at her computer doing her dream job—creating the romances she loves. Visit Nicola's Web site at www.nicolamarsh.com for the latest news of her books.

Get swept away
by Harlequin® Romance's new miniseries

Dream destinations, whirlwind weddings!

Let us take you on a whirlwind tour of the globe,
stopping at stunning, exotic and mysterious places—
dream destinations in which to fall in love.

From glorious beaches to towns buzzing with
activity and culture, every setting is glamorous,
colorful and, most importantly, sets the scene
for a beautiful romance!

Next stop: soak up the sun in gorgeous
Greece with Rebecca Winters in
The Greek's Long-Lost Son
October 2009

Then travel through magical China
with Lucy Gordon in
And the Bride Wore Red
December 2009

CHAPTER ONE

TAMARA RAYNE'S high heels clacked impatiently against the cobblestones as she strode towards Ambrosia, Melbourne's hippest restaurant, a gourmet's delight and the place where she was trying to get her life back on track.

Her favourite butterscotch boots, patent leather with a towering heel—impractical yet gorgeous—never failed to invoke the stuff of her surname as plump drops splashed down from the heavens and lashed her in a stinging sheet.

With her laden arms and no umbrella, she needed a mythical knight in shining armour. She'd thought she'd had him once in Richard. How wrong she'd been.

Blinking back futile tears—wasted tears, angry tears—she pushed on Ambrosia's door with her behind, staggering with her load, almost slamming into her knight.

More of a pirate, really, a corporate pirate in a designer suit with rain-slicked dark hair, roguish blue eyes and a devilish smile.

'Need a hand?'

Definitely devilish, and used to great effect if the constant parade of women traipsing through Ethan Brooks's life was any indication.

'You're back.'

'Miss me?'

'Hardly.'

She hadn't meant to sound so frosty but then, what was he doing? Flirting? She barely knew him, had seen him three times in the last year out of necessity, so why the familiarity?

'Too bad.' He shrugged, his roguish smile widening as he pointed to the bundle in her arms. 'Do you want help with that?'

Quashing the urge to take her load and run, she nodded. 'Thanks.'

He grunted as she offloaded the bag perched precariously on top of the rest. 'What's in here? Bricks for the new tandoori oven I've ordered?'

'Almost as heavy.'

Her voice wobbled, just a tad, and she swallowed, twice. It was the mention of the tandoori oven that did it.

Her mum had loved tandoori chicken, had scored the chicken to let the spices and yoghurt marinate into it, had painstakingly threaded the pieces onto skewers before grilling, while lamenting the loss of her real oven back in Goa.

Her mother had missed her homeland so much, despite living in Melbourne for the last thirty years of her life. It had been the reason they'd planned their special trip together: a trip back in time for her mum, a trip to open Tamara's eyes to a culture she'd never known even though Indian blood ran in her veins.

Thanks to Richard, the trip never happened and, while her mum had died three years ago and she'd come to terms with her grief, she'd never forgiven him for robbing her of that precious experience.

Now, more than ever, she needed her mum, missed her terribly. Khushi would've been her only ally, would've been the only one she trusted with the truth about Richard, and would've helped her reclaim her identity, her life.

Hot, bitter tears of regret stung her eyes and she deliberately glanced over Ethan's shoulder, focusing on anything other than the curiosity in his eyes.

'Can you take the rest? My arms are killing me.'

She knew he wouldn't push, wouldn't ask her what was wrong.

He hadn't pushed when she'd been detached and withdrawn following Richard's death while they'd sorted through the legal rigmarole of the restaurant.

He hadn't pushed when she'd approached him to use Ambrosia six months ago to kick-start her career.

Instead, he'd taken an extended business trip, had been aloof as always. There was a time she'd thought he disliked her, such was his distant demeanour whenever she entered a room.

But she hadn't wasted time figuring it out. He was Richard's mate and that was all the reason she needed to keep her distance. Ethan, like the rest of the planet, thought Richard was great: top chef, top entertainer, top bloke.

If they only knew.

'Sure.' He took the bulk of her load, making it look easy as he held the door open. 'Coming in?'

She didn't need to be asked twice as she stepped into the only place she called home these days.

Ambrosia: food of the gods. More like food for her soul.

It had become her refuge, her safe haven the last few months. Crazy, considering Richard had owned part of it, had been head chef since its inception, and they'd met here when she'd come to critique Melbourne's latest culinary hot spot.

For that alone she should hate the place.

But the welcoming warmth of Ambrosia, with its polished honey oak boards, brick fireplace and comfy cushioned chairs that had drawn her here every Monday for the last six months was hard to resist and what better place for a food critic determined to return to the workforce to practise her trade?

Throw in the best hot chocolate this side of the Yarra and she couldn't stay away.

As she dumped her remaining load on a nearby table and

stretched her aching arms, her gaze drifted to the enigmatic man lighting a match to kindling in the fireplace.

What was he doing here?

From all accounts, Ethan was unpredictable, blew hotter and colder than a Melbourne spring breeze. His employees enjoyed working here but never knew when the imperturbable, ruthless businessman would appear.

She'd been happy to have the place to herself the last six months, other than the skilled staff and eager patrons who poured through the door of course, had been strangely uncomfortable the few times she and Ethan met.

There was something about him...an underlying steeliness, a hard streak, an almost palpable electricity that buzzed and crackled, indicative of a man in command, a man on top of his game and intent on staying there.

He straightened and she quickly averted her gaze, surprised to find it had been lingering on a piece of his anatomy she had no right noticing.

She'd never done that—noticed him as a man. He was Richard's business partner, someone who'd always been distantly polite to her the few times their paths had crossed, but that was it.

So why the quick flush of heat, the flicker of guilt?

It had been a year since Richard's death, two since she'd been touched by a man, which went a long way to explaining her wandering gaze. She may be numb on the inside, emotionally anaesthetised, but she wasn't dead and any woman with a pulse would've checked out Ethan's rather impressive rear end.

'If I get you a drink, will you tell me what's in the bags?'

Slipping out of her camel trench coat, she slung it onto the back of a chair. She didn't want to tell him, didn't want to show him the culmination of half a year's work.

She'd come here for privacy, for inspiration, and having him here intruded on that. Ridiculous, considering he owned the place and could come and go as he pleased, but something about his greeting had rankled, something about that damn smile.

'I'd kill for a hot chocolate, thanks.'

'Coming right up.'

His gaze lingered on the bags before meeting hers, challenging. 'I won't give up until I know what's in there so why don't you just tell me?'

He stared at her, unflinching, direct, his persistence indicative of a guy used to getting his own way, a guy who demanded nothing less.

She fingered the hessian holding her future, *mind your own business* hovering on her lips. His authority niggled, grated, but he'd given her the opportunity to relaunch her career by using this place and she should be civil if nothing else.

'If you throw in a side of marshmallows, I'll show you.'

'You're on.'

With a half salute and a twinkle in his eyes, he strode towards the bar.

Ah…the pirate was in top form today. Full of swagger, cheek and suave bravado. She was immune to his charm, of course, but for a split second it felt good, great, in fact, to be on the receiving end of some of that legendary charm.

While he headed for the espresso machine behind the bar she plopped onto a chair, stretched her legs and wiggled her toes. She loved these boots, she really did, but they were nothing but trouble for the weather, her feet and her back, which gave a protesting twinge as she sat up.

Though that could be more to do with the ten-ton load she'd hefted up the street, but she'd had no choice. She held her future in her hands—literally—and, despite the gut feeling she was ready for this, it wouldn't hurt to get Ethan's opinion on it. If anyone knew this business inside out, he did.

'Here you go. One hot chocolate with a double side of marshmallows.'

He placed the towering glass in front of her, a strong Americano in front of him, and slid into the chair opposite, fixing her with a half-amused, half-laconic tilt of his lips.

'I've kept my side of the bargain, so come on, what's in there?'

'A girl can't think without a sip of chocolate first.'

She cradled the mug, inhaled the rich chocolate-fragrant steam, savoured the warmth seeping into her palms and, closing her eyes, took a deep sip, letting the sweet lusciousness glide over her taste buds and slide down her throat.

Ethan made a strange sound and her eyes flew open, confused by the flicker of something darker, mysterious in his eyes before he quickly masked it.

'Right. One sip, you said.' He tapped the nearest bag. 'Now, let's have it.'

'You hotshot businessmen are all the same. Way too impatient.'

She placed her mug on the table, unzipping the first bag and hauling out a folder.

He tilted his head on an angle to read the spine. 'What's that?'

'A list of every restaurant in Melbourne. The new list I've been compiling over the last six months.'

Her tummy quivered as she glanced at the folder, at what it meant for her future.

'I'm ready.'

His eyes sparked with understanding and she wondered how he could do that. He'd read her mind, whereas Richard hadn't a clue what she'd been thinking after three years of marriage. Then again, considering what he'd been up to, he probably hadn't cared.

'You're going back to work?'

'Uh-huh. Thanks to your chef whipping up those amazing meals and letting me get my hand back into critiquing, I reckon I'm finally ready.'

She gnawed on her bottom lip, worrying it till she tasted the gloss she'd swiped on this morning.

'Think I'm crazy?'

His eyebrows shot up. 'Crazy? I think it's brilliant. Just what you need, something to focus on, get your mind off losing Rich.'

She hated the pity in his eyes, hated the fact she still had to fake grief, still had to pretend she cared.

She didn't.

Not since that first incident four months into her marriage when the man she'd married had given her a frightening glimpse into her future.

She'd thought Richard was the type of guy to never let her down, the type of guy to keep her safe, to give her what she'd always wanted: stability, security—something she'd never had since her dad had died when she was ten.

But Richard hadn't been that guy and, from the accolades of his adoring public and coworkers, she was the only one who knew the truth.

That Richard Downey, Australia's premier celebrity chef, had been an out-and-out bastard. And it was times like this, when she had to pretend in front of one of his mates, that an all-consuming latent fury swept through her.

If he hadn't upped and died of a heart attack, she would've been tempted to kill him herself for what he'd put her through, and what she'd discovered after his death.

'This has nothing to do with Richard. I'm doing it for me.'

Her bitterness spilled out in a torrent and she clamped her lips shut. He didn't deserve to bear the brunt of her resentment towards Richard. She'd wasted enough time analysing and self-flagellating and fuelling her anger. That was all she'd been doing for the last year since he'd died—speculating, brooding over a whole lot of pointless 'what-ifs'.

What if she'd known about the affair?

What if she'd stood up to him and for herself, rather than keeping up appearances for the sake of his business?

What if she'd travelled to India with her mum when Khushi had first asked her years ago? Would any of that have changed her life for the better?

'I didn't mean to rehash any painful stuff for you.'

Shaking her head, she wished the simple action could wipe away her awful memories.

'Not your fault. It's not like I don't think about it every day anyway.'

He searched her face for—what? Confirmation she wasn't still grieving, wasn't so heartbroken she couldn't return to the workforce after wasting the last few years playing society hostess to a man who hadn't given a damn about her?

What he saw in her expression had his eyes narrowing in speculation.

'You should get away. A break, before you get sucked back into the full-time rat race. Take it from me, a certified workaholic, once you hit the ground running you won't have a minute to yourself.'

She opened her mouth to protest, to tell him that as a virtual stranger he could stick his advice, but he held a finger to her lips to silence her, the impact of his simple action slugging her all the way to her toes. It had to be the impulse to tell him to shut up rather than the brush of his finger against her lips causing her belly to twist like a pretzel.

'A piece of advice. Seeing you six months ago, seeing you now, you've held together remarkably well considering what you've been through, but it's time.'

He dropped his finger, thank goodness.

'For what?'

'Time for *you*. Time to put aside your grief. Move on.'

He gestured to the stack of folders on the table between them. 'From what I've heard, you're a damn good food critic, one of Melbourne's best. But honestly? The way you are right now, the tears I saw when I made a simple flyaway comment about an oven, what you just said about thinking about Rich every day, holding down a regular job would be tough. You'd end up not being able to tell the difference between steak tartare and well-done Wagyu beef, let alone write about it.'

She should hate him for what he'd just said. It hurt, all of it. But then, the truth often did.

'You finished?'

She knew it was the wrong thing to say to a guy like him — the instant the words left her mouth, for it sounded like a challenge, something he would never back away from.

'Not by a long shot.'

Before she could blink, his mouth swooped, capturing hers in a heartbeat—a soul-reviving, soul-destroying, terrifying kiss that stirred her dormant body to life, setting it alight in a way she'd never dreamed possible.

She burned, swayed, as he changed the pressure, his lips coaxing a response—a response she couldn't give in her right mind.

But she wasn't in her right mind, hadn't been from the second his lips touched hers and, before she could think, rationalise, overanalyse, she kissed him back, an outpouring of pent-up passion from a shattered ego starving for an ounce of attention.

Her heart sang with the joy of it, before stalling as the implication of what she'd just done crashed over her in a sickening wave.

Ethan, the practised playboy, Richard's friend, a guy she barely knew, had kissed her.

And she'd let him.

Slivers of ice chilled her to the bone as she tore her mouth from his, staring at him in wide-eyed horror.

She couldn't speak, couldn't form the words to express how furious she was with him.

Though her anger was misplaced and she knew it. She was furious with herself for responding; worse, for enjoying it.

'Don't expect me to apologise for that.'

His eyes glittered with desire and she shivered, petrified yet exhilarated to be the focus of all that passion for a passing moment in time.

'That should show you you're a vibrant woman who needs to start living again. You should start by doing one thing you've always wanted to do before you return to work.'

He made sense, damn him, prove-a-point kiss and all. And while her body still trembled from the impact of that alarming kiss and her astounding response, at least it had served a purpose. If she'd been prevaricating about taking a trip before, he'd blasted her doubts sky-high now.

She had to go, had to leave Ambrosia, for facing him in the future would be beyond mortifying.

Mustering a haughty glare that only served to make his eyes gleam more, she shook her head.

'I can't believe you just did that.'

Shrugging, he sat back and crossed his ankles, the supremely confident male and proud of it. 'Many people can't believe a lot of the stuff I do, so don't sweat it. Let's talk about this trip of yours.'

'Let's not,' she snapped, annoyed by his persistence, more annoyed by the glimmer of anticipation racing through her.

She'd already been thinking about a trip herself. Specifically, the trip she'd booked with her mum. The itinerary they'd planned was tucked away in her old music box at home, the one her dad had given her when she'd been three, the one with the haunting tune that never failed to make her cry when she thought of all she'd lost.

She'd contemplated taking the trip on her own for all of two seconds before slamming the idea. The trip would've been emotional enough with her mum by her side but without her?

Her eyelids prickled just thinking about it and she blinked, wishing Ethan would put that devilish smile to good use elsewhere and butt out of her business.

'Think sun, sand and surf. Somewhere hot, tropical, the opposite of blustery Melbourne at the moment.'

Considering her toes were icy within her boots and she couldn't feel her fingers, the thought of all that heat was tempting.

India would be perfect, would fit the bill in every way. Buoyed by an urge to escape, she rummaged through the top folder, wondering if a brochure was still there. She'd had hundreds of the things when they'd been planning the trip, immersing herself in India, from the stone-walled city of Jodhpur—home of the Mehrangarh Fort and the grand palaces of Moti Mahal, Sheesh Mahal, Phool Mahal, Sileh Khana and Daulat Khana—to Ranthambhore National Park, India's best wildlife sanctuary, to see the majestic tigers, eager to see as much of the intriguing country as possible.

She'd kept them everywhere, hiding them from Richard when he'd first expressed his displeasure at letting her out of his sight, tucking them into books and magazines and her work stuff.

Suddenly, she really wanted to find one, wanted to see if the tiny flame of excitement flickering to life could be fanned into her actually doing this.

Flicking to the front of the folder, she dug her fingers into the plastic pocket and almost yelled for joy when she pulled out a glossy brochure featuring the Taj Mahal and the legendary Palace on Wheels train on the front.

'You're one of those incredibly annoying, painfully persistent guys who won't give up, so here. Take a look.'

She handed him the brochure.

His eyes widened. 'India?'

'I planned to visit a few years ago but it never happened.' She stared at the brochure, captivated by the exoticism of it all.

She should've thrown this out ages ago, but as long as she hung onto it, as long as the promise of her mum's dream trip was still a reality, albeit a distant one, it was as if she were keeping alive her mum's spirit.

Every time she found a brochure tucked away somewhere she felt connected to her mum, remembering the day she'd picked them up as a sixtieth birthday surprise and they'd pored over them during an Indian feast of spicy, palate-searing beef vindaloo, masala prawns, parathas and biryani, her favourite spiced rice, rich in flavoursome lamb.

They'd laughed, they'd cried, they'd hugged each other and jumped up and down like a couple of excited kids heading away on their first camping trip.

She'd wanted to explore the part of her history she knew little about, wanted to take the special journey with her mum.

Richard may have put paid to that dream and, while she'd love to take the trip now, it just wouldn't be the same without Khushi.

'Guess I should explore all my options first.'

She fiddled with the brochure, folding the ends into tiny triangles, absentmindedly smoothing out the creases again.

'Uh-uh.' He snapped his fingers. 'You're going to take the trip.'

Her eyes flew to his, startled by his absolute conviction, as a lump of sorrow lodged in her throat and she cleared it. 'I can't.'

She'd find another destination, somewhere she wouldn't have a deluge of memories drowning her, missing her mum every step of the way.

He stabbed at the brochure. 'You can. Clear your head, make a fresh start.'

She shook her head, using her hair to shield her face. 'I can't do this trip alone. I'd planned to take it with my mum. This was her trip—'

Her voice cracked and she slid off her chair and headed for the fireplace, holding her hands out to the crackling warmth, wishing it could seep deep inside to the coldest, loneliest parts of her soul.

'You won't be alone.'

He came up behind her, the heat from the fire nothing on the warmth radiating from him—a solid, welcoming warmth she wished she could lean into before giving herself a swift mental slap.

Stepping around in front of her, he stared at her, direct, intense, the indigo flecks in his blue eyes gleaming in the reflected firelight.

'You won't be alone because I'm coming with you.'

'But—'

'No buts.'

He held up a hand. 'I'm going to India anyway, to lure Delhi's best chef to work here.'

One finger bent as he counted off his first point.

'You need company.'

The second finger went down.

'And, lastly, I've always wanted to do the Palace on Wheels trip and never got around to it so, this way, you're doing me a favour.'

Her eyes narrowed. 'How's that?'

'I hear it's an amazing journey, best shared with a beautiful companion.'

His smile could've lit the Arts Centre spire, damn pirate, and in that second she snapped to her senses.

What was she doing? He'd be the last person she'd take a trip with, the last guy to accompany her anywhere considering he'd just kissed her and turned some of that legendary charm onto her. Beautiful companion, indeed.

'Your mum would've wanted you to go.'

Oh, he was good.

Worse, he was right.

Khushi would've wanted her to go, to visit Goa and the

beach where she'd met her father, to take a magical train journey through India's heartland, to visit the Taj Mahal, something her mum had craved her entire life.

She wanted to rediscover her identity. Maybe a link to her past was the best way to do it?

Staggered by her second impulse in as many minutes—she determinedly ignored the first, foolishly responding to that kiss—she slapped the brochure against her opposite palm, mind made up.

'You're right, I'm taking the trip.'

She fixed him with a glare that lost its impact when her lower lip wobbled at the enormity of what she was contemplating.

'That's great. We'll—'

'I'm taking the trip. *Alone.*'

'But—'

'I don't even know you,' she said, wishing she hadn't stayed, terrified how that incredible kiss had made her feel for a fleeting moment.

It had obviously given him the wrong idea. What sort of a guy went from a cool acquaintance to kissing her to thinking she'd go away with him?

Maybe she was overreacting, reading more into the sudden twinkle in his sea-blue eyes and his scarily sexy smile?

Leaning forward a fraction, invading her personal space with a potent masculinity she found disconcerting, he lowered his voice. 'That's what the trip is for. Loads of time to get to know one another.'

She wasn't overreacting. He was chatting her up!

Sending him a withering glance that would've extinguished the fire at her back, she headed for the table and slipped her trench coat on.

'Thanks for the offer but I like being on my own.'

When he opened his mouth to respond, she held up a hand. 'I like it that way.'

Before he could protest any further, she slung her bag over her shoulder and pointed to the stack of folders. 'I'll come back for these tomorrow.'

His knowing gaze followed her towards the door and she knew he'd get the last word in.

'Going solo is highly overrated.'

Halting with her hand on the door, she glanced over her shoulder, startled by the ravenous hunger in his greedy gaze.

'Someone like you would think that.'

Rather than annoying him, a triumphant grin lit his face, as if she'd just paid him a compliment.

'Next to business, dating is what I do best so I guess that makes me qualified to pass judgement.'

'Overqualified, from what I hear.'

His grin widened and she mentally clapped a hand over her mouth.

What was she doing, discussing his personal life? It had nothing to do with her and, while she valued the opportunity he'd given her in using Ambrosia as a base to relaunch her career, what he did in his spare time meant diddly-squat to her.

Propped against the bar, he appeared more like a pirate than ever: all he needed was a bandanna and eye patch to complete the overconfident look.

'You sure you wouldn't like me to tag along?'

'Positive.'

She walked out, somewhat satisfied by the slamming door.

Take a trip with a playboy pirate like Ethan Brooks?

She'd rather walk the plank.

CHAPTER TWO

'WHAT the hell are you doing here?'

Ethan grinned at Tamara's shell-shocked expression as he strolled towards her on the platform at Safdarjung Station.

'You mean here as in New Delhi or here as in this station?'

Her eyes narrowed, spitting emerald fire. 'Don't play smart with me. Why are you here?'

'Business. I told you I'm a workaholic. The Delhi chef wasn't interested so there's a chef in Udaipur I'd like to lure to Ambrosia. Rather than commute by boring planes I thought I'd take the scenic route, so here I am.'

By her folded arms, compressed lips and frown, she wasn't giving an inch.

'And this *business trip* just happened to coincide when I'm taking the trip. How convenient.'

'Pure coincidence.'

He couldn't keep the grin off his face, which only served to rile her further. That smile may well have seduced every socialite in Melbourne, but she wasn't about to succumb to its practised charm. He laid a hand on her arm; she stiffened and deliberately stepped away.

'If it makes you feel any better, it's a big train and the trip only lasts a week.'

'It doesn't make me feel better.'

If the Tamara he'd seen all too infrequently over the last few years was beautiful, a furious Tamara was stunning—and vindicated why he'd booked this trip in the first place.

It was time.

He was through waiting.

'Why don't we stop quibbling and enjoy this fanfare?'

He thought she'd never relent but, after shooting him another exasperated glare, she turned towards their welcoming committee.

'Pretty impressive, huh?'

She nodded, maintaining a silence he found disconcerting. He preferred her annoyed and fiery rather than quiet and brooding.

Only one way to get her out of this huff. Turn on the charm.

'Just think, all this for you. Talented musicians playing tabla as you board the train, young Indian girls placing flower garlands around your neck, being greeted by your own personal bearer for your carriage. Nothing like a proper welcome?'

The beginnings of a smile softened her lips as a bearer placed a fancy red turban on his head as a gift.

'Looks like I'm not the only one getting welcomed.'

He wobbled his head, doing a precarious balancing act with the turban and she finally laughed.

'Okay, you can stay.'

He executed a fancy little bow and she held up a hand.

'But remember I like being on my own.'

He didn't. Being alone was highly overrated and something he'd set about compensating for the moment he'd had his first pay cheque or two.

He liked being surrounded by people, enjoyed the bustle of a restaurant, thrived on the hub of the business world and relished dating beautiful women. Most of all, he liked being in control. And, finally, this was his chance to take control of his desire for Tamara.

He'd kept his distance while Rich was alive, had respected

his friend's marriage. But Rich was gone and his pull towards this incredible woman was stronger than ever.

He wanted her, had wanted her from the first moment they'd met and had avoided her because of it.

Not any more.

That impulsive kiss had changed everything.

He'd forfeited control by giving in to his driving compulsion for her, hated the powerlessness she'd managed to wreak with her startling response, and he'd be damned if he sat back and did nothing.

Having her walk away had left her firmly in charge and that was unacceptable. He was here to reclaim control, to prove he couldn't lose it over a woman, beautiful as she may be.

Seduction was one thing, but finding himself floundering by the power of a kiss quite another.

Clawing his way to the top had taught him persistence, determination and diligence. When he wanted something in the business world, he made it happen by dogged perseverance and a healthy dose of charm.

Now, he wanted Tamara.

She didn't stand a chance.

Tapping his temple, he said, 'I'll try to remember. But, you know, this heat can play havoc with one's memory and—'

'Come on, let's board. Once you're safely ensconced in the lap of luxury, maybe that memory will return.'

'You make me sound like a snob.'

'Aren't you? Being Australia's top restaurateur and all.' She snapped her fingers. 'Oh, that's right. You're just the average run-of-the-mill billionaire who happens to rival Wolfgang Puck and Nobu for top restaurants around the world. Nothing snobby about you.'

'Come on, funny girl. Time to board.'

She smiled and, as he picked up their hand luggage and followed the porter, he could hardly believe the change in Tam.

Sure, there was still a hint of fragility about her, the glimpse of sorrow clinging to her like the humidity here, but it looked as if India agreed with her. After she'd finished berating him, she'd smiled more in the last few minutes than she had in the odd times he'd seen her.

'You know I have my own compartment?'

She rolled her eyes. 'Of course.'

'I wouldn't want you compromising my reputation.'

She smiled again and something twanged in the vicinity of his heart. She'd had the ability to do that to him from the very beginning, from the first time he'd met her—an hour after she'd met Richard. worse luck.

She'd been smitten by then, with eyes only for the loud, larger-than-life chef, and he'd subdued his controlling instincts to sweep her away.

Neither of them had ever known of his desire for the woman he couldn't have; he'd made sure of it. But keeping his distance was a thing of the past and the next seven days loomed as intriguing.

'Your reputation is safe with me. I'm sure all those society heiresses and vapid, thin models you date on a revolving-door basis are well aware this boring old widow is no competition.'

'You're not boring and you're certainly not old.'

As for the women he dated, there was a reason he chose the no-commitment, out-for-a-good-time-not-a-long-time type. A damn good one.

The smile hovering about her lips faded as fast as his hopes to keep it there.

'But I am a widow.'

And, while he'd hated the pain she must've gone through after Rich died, the struggle to get her life back on an even keel, he couldn't help but be glad she was now single.

Did that make him heartless? Maybe, but his past had taught him to be a realist and he never wasted time lying to himself or others. Discounting the way he'd kept his attraction for Tam a secret all these years, of course.

'Maybe it's time you came out of mourning?'

He expected her to recoil, to send him the contemptuous stare she'd given him after he'd kissed her. Instead, she cocked her head to one side, studying him.

'Are you always this blunt?'

'Always.'

'So you'll ignore me if I tell you to butt out, just like you did by gatecrashing my trip?'

He feigned hurt, smothering his grin with difficulty. 'Gatecrashing's a bit harsh. I told you, I'm here on business.'

He only just caught her muttered, 'Monkey business.'

She fidgeted with her handbag, her fingers plucking at the leather strap as she rocked her weight from foot to foot, and he almost took pity on her before banishing that uncharacteristic emotion in a second.

He had to have her, was driven by a primal urge he had no control over and, to do that, he needed to get her to look at him as a man rather than a bug in her soup.

With a bit of luck and loads of charm, he intended to make good on the unspoken promise of their first kiss—a promise of so much more.

'You're not still hung up over that kiss, are you? Because, if you are—'

'I'm not. It's forgotten.'

Her gorgeous blush belied her quick negation and had him itching to push the boundaries. But he'd gained ground by having her accept his presence so quickly and he'd be a fool to take things too far on the first day.

'Forgotten, huh? Must be losing my touch.'

'There's nothing wrong with—'

He smothered a triumphant grin. He may have lost his mind and kissed her to prove she needed to start living again but her eager response had blown him away. And fuelled his need for her, driving him to crazy things like taking time off work, something he rarely did, to pursue her.

'Let's put it down to a distant memory and move on, shall we?'

To his horror, her eyes filled with pain, which hit him hard, like a slug to the guts, and he tugged her close without thinking, enveloping her in his arms.

'Hell, Tam, I'm sorry. I shouldn't have mentioned memories.'

She braced herself against his chest, her palms splayed, and his body reacted in an instant, heat searing his veins as he cradled a soft armful of woman.

She sniffled and he tightened his hold, rather than his first instinct to release her in the hope of putting an instant dampener on his errant libido.

His hand skimmed her hair, thick and dark like molten molasses, soothing strokes designed to comfort. But, hot on the heels of his thoughts of how much he wanted her, his fingers itched to delve into the shiny, dark mass and get caught up in it. He could hold her like this all night long.

'You okay?'

Ethan pulled away, needing to establish some distance between them, not liking her power over him. He didn't do comfort. He never had a hankie in his pocket or a host of placating platitudes or a shoulder to cry on. He didn't do consoling hugs; he did passionate embraces.

So what had happened in the last few minutes? What was it about this woman that undermined him?

'Uh-huh.'

She managed a watery smile before straightening her shoulders and lifting her head in the classic coping pose he'd seen her exhibit at Rich's funeral and his admiration shot up another few notches.

How she'd handled her grief after the initial shock of Rich's heart attack, burying herself in the business side of things, sorting through legalities with him, only to approach him several months later for the use of Ambrosia to get her career back on track, had all served to fuel his respect for this amazing woman.

Quite simply, she was incredible and he wanted her with a staggering fierceness that clawed at him even now, when he was left analysing how he'd let his control slip again in her intoxicating presence.

'I can see you're still hurting but if you ever want to talk about Rich, remember the good times, I'm here for you, okay?'

Maybe, if she opened up to him, he could encourage her to get it all out of her system and move on. Highly altruistic but then, when was he anything but?

To his surprise, she wrinkled her nose and he knew it had little to do with the pungent odours of diesel fumes, spices and human sweat swirling around them.

'Honestly? I don't want to talk about Richard. I'm done grieving.'

A spark of defiance lit her eyes, turning them from soft moss-green to sizzling emerald in a second. 'I want to enjoy this trip, then concentrate on my future.'

He'd never seen her like this: resolute, determined, a woman reborn.

He'd seen Tam the society wife, the perfect hostess, the astute businesswoman, the grieving widow, but never like this and a part of him was glad. Releasing the past was cathartic, would help her to move on and he really wanted her to do that on this trip. With him.

'Sounds like a plan.'

Her answering smile sent another sizzle of heat through him and he clenched his hands to stop himself from reaching out and pulling her close.

Plenty of time for that.

* * *

Tamara lay down on the bed, stretched her arms over her head and smiled.

The rocking motion of the train, the clickety-clack as it bounced its way out of Delhi, the aroma of marigolds and masala chai—the delicious tea, fragrant with cardamons—overloaded her senses, lulled her while making her want to jump up and twirl around from the sheer rush of it.

For the first time in years, she felt free. Free to do whatever she wanted, be whoever she chose. And it felt great. In fact, it felt downright fantastic.

While she'd once loved Richard, had desperately craved the type of marriage her folks had had, nothing came close to this exhilarating freedom.

She'd spent months playing the grieving widow after Richard had suffered that fatal heart attack, had submerged her humiliation, her bitterness, her pain.

Yet behind her serene, tear-stained face she'd seethed: at him for making a mockery of their marriage, at herself for being a gullible fool and for caring what people thought even after he was gone.

She hadn't given two hoots about social propriety until she'd married him, had laughed at his obsession with appearances. But she'd soon learned he was serious and, with his face plastered over every newspaper, magazine and TV channel on a regular basis, she'd slipped into the routine of being the perfect little wife he'd wanted.

While his perfect little mistress had been stashed away in a luxurious beach house at Cape Schanck, just over an hour's drive from Melbourne's CBD where they'd lived.

Damn him.

She sat bolt upright, annoyed she'd let bitter memories tarnish the beginning of this incredible journey, her gaze falling on the single bed next to hers. The single bed her mum should've been occupying while regaling her with exotic tales of Goa and its beaches, Colva beach where she'd met her dad, her love at first sight for a scruffy Aussie backpacker with a twinkle in his eyes and a ready smile.

Tales of the Taj Mahal, the monument she'd always wanted to see but never had the chance. Tales of an India filled with hospitable people and mouth-watering food, imparting recipes in that lilting sing-song accent that had soothed her as a young girl when the nightmares of losing her dad would wake her screaming and sweat-drenched.

Khushi should've been here. This was her trip.

Instead, Tamara swiped an angry hand across her eyes, dashing her tears away.

She wasn't going to cry any more. She'd made herself that promise back in Melbourne when she'd decided to take this trip.

And while she knew her heart would break at every turn on the track, at every fabulous place she visited, wishing her mum was here to share it with her, she should be thankful she'd taken another positive step in getting her life in order.

She was through cringing with shame and humiliation at what Richard had put her through, done feeling sorry for herself.

This was *her* time.

Time for a new life, a new beginning.

So what the heck was Ethan Brooks doing here, muscling in on her new start?

Ethan, with his smiling eyes and that deadly smile. Where was the famed hard-ass, hard-nosed businessman? Instead, Ethan the pirate, the player, the playboy, had swaggered along on this trip and while every self-preservation instinct screamed for her to stay away, she couldn't be that rude.

He'd helped her with the legalities surrounding Ambrosia after Richard's death, had smoothed the way for her to re-enter the workforce by allowing her to use Ambrosia as a base. She owed him.

But he had her rattled.

She preferred him business-oriented, juggling a briefcase, a laptop and barking instructions on a mobile phone at the same time, barely acknowledging her presence with an absentminded nod as he strutted into Ambrosia.

He'd practically ignored her when their paths had crossed while Richard had been around, his head always buried in financial statements and yearly projections, and that had been fine with her.

He made her uncomfortable and it had nothing to do with the fact that they didn't really know each other. The shift had happened when they'd met to sort out Ambrosia's ownership, those two times when she'd noticed things: like the way he cracked pistachio nuts way too loudly, flipping them in the air and catching them in his open mouth, how much he loved Shiraz Grenache and sticky date pudding and the North Melbourne Football Club.

Trivial things, inconsequential things that meant little, but the fact that she'd noticed and remembered them annoyed her.

As for that kiss…she picked up a pillow and smothered a groan, hating how it haunted her, hating how she'd dreamed of it, hating how the dream had developed and morphed into so much more than a kiss, leaving her writhing and panting and sweat-drenched on waking.

She didn't want to remember any of it, didn't want to remember his expertise, his spontaneity, his ability to dredge a response from her deepest, darkest soul, better left untouched.

But she did remember, every breathtaking moment, and while her head had slammed the door on the memory of her temporary insanity, her body was clamouring for more.

Now this.

Him being here, all suave and charming and too gorgeous for his own good, was making her nervous. Very nervous.

She didn't need anyone in her new life, least of all a smooth tycoon like Ethan Brooks.

As for her wayward thoughts lately in the wee small hours of the morning when she lay sleepless, staring up at the ceiling and trying to regain focus to her meandering life, she'd banish them along with her anger at Richard.

Wondering what would've happened if she'd gone for Ethan rather than Richard that fateful night she'd entered Ambrosia four years earlier was a waste of time.

Now was her chance to put the past to rest and concentrate on her future.

CHAPTER THREE

'TELL me you're not working.'

Ethan pointed at the small blue notebook tucked discreetly under her linen serviette—obviously not discreetly enough.

Ignoring him, Tamara sliced a vegetable pakora in two and dipped it in the tamarind sauce, her taste buds hankering for that first delicious taste of crispy vegetables battered in chickpea flour and dunked in the sour, piquant sauce.

'Fine, I won't tell you.'

He shook his head, laughed, before helping himself to a meat samosa from the entrée platter between them.

'You're supposed to be on holiday.'

'I'm supposed to be getting back to work soon and I need the practice.'

Resting his knife and fork on his plate, he focused his too-blue gaze on her.

'You're an expert critic. One of Australia's best. Skills like that don't disappear because you've had a year or so off.'

'Two years,' she said, quelling the surge of resentment at what she'd given up for Richard. 'Despite the last six months at Ambrosia, I'm still rusty. The sooner I get back into it, the easier it'll be.'

She bit down on the pakora, chewed thoughtfully, knowing

there was another reason she had her trusty notebook within jotting reach.

The minute she'd opened her compartment door to find Ethan on the other side in charcoal casual pants and open-necked white shirt, his gaze appreciative and his smile as piratical as always, she'd had to clamp down on the irrational urge to slam the door in his face and duck for cover.

It had been her stupid thoughts earlier of *what if* that had done it, that had made her aware of him as a man—a gorgeous, charming man—rather than just her…what was he? A business acquaintance? A travelling companion? A friend?

She didn't like the last two options: they implied a closeness she didn't want. But they'd moved past the acquaintance stage the moment he'd kissed her and there was no going back.

She didn't want to have these thoughts, didn't want to acknowledge the sexy crease in his left cheek, the tiny lines at the corners of his eyes that added character to his face, the endearingly ruffled dark hair that curled over his collar.

She'd never noticed those things before or, if she had, hadn't experienced this…this…*buzz* or whatever the strange feeling coursing through her body was that made her want to bury her nose in her notebook for the duration of dinner and not look up.

That might take care of day one, but what about the rest of the week as the Palace on Wheels took them on an amazing journey through Rajasthan?

Ethan was Richard's friend, reason enough she couldn't trust him, no matter how much he poured on the charm.

She'd fallen for Richard because he'd been safe and look at the devastation he'd wreaked. What would letting her guard down around a powerful, compelling guy like Ethan do?

Inwardly shuddering at the thought, she reached for the notebook at the same instant that he stilled her hand. Her gaze flew to his, her heart beating uncharacteristically fast.

He'd touched her again. First that hug on the station and now this. Though this time her pulse tripped and her skin prickled as determination flared in his eyes, while fear crept through her.

Fear they'd somehow changed the boundaries of their nebulous relationship without realising, fear they could never go back, fear she could lose focus of what she wanted out of this trip and why if she was crazy enough to acknowledge the shift between them, let alone do anything about it.

'This is the first holiday you've taken in years. Don't be so hard on yourself.'

He squeezed her hand, released it and she exhaled, unaware she'd been holding her breath.

'You'll get back into the swing of things soon enough. Once I coerce the super-talented Indian chef to leave the Lake Palace and work at Ambrosia, critiquing his meals will keep you busy for months.'

'You're too kind.'

She meant it. He'd never been anything other than kind to her, helping her with Richard's business stuff, arranging a special table for her at Ambrosia away from the ravenous crowd so she could sample the food and write her critiques in peace.

But kind didn't come close to describing the hungry gleam in his eyes or the subtle shift that had taken place between them a few moments ago—dangerous, more like it. Dangerous and exciting and terrifying.

He screwed up his nose, stabbing a seekh kebab from the entrée platter and moving it across to his plate. 'You know, *kind* ranks right up there with *nice* for guys. Something we don't want to hear.'

'Fine. You're a cold, heartless businessman who takes no prisoners. Better?'

'Much.'

His bold smile had her scrambling for her notebook,

flipping it open to a crisp new blank page, pen poised. 'Now, take a bite of that kebab and tell me what you think.'

He cut the kebab—spiced lamb moulded into a sausage shape around a skewer and cooked to perfection in a tandoor oven—and chewed a piece, emitting a satisfied moan that had her focusing on his lips rather than her notebook.

'Fantastic.'

He screwed up his eyes, took another bite, chewed thoughtfully. 'I can taste ginger, a hint of garlic and cumin.'

He polished off the rest with a satisfied pat of his tummy, a very lean, taut tummy from what she could see of it outlined beneath his shirt.

Great, there she went again, noticing things she never normally would. This wasn't good—not good at all.

Pressing the pen to the page so hard it tore a hole through to the paper underneath, she focused on her scrawl rather than anywhere in the vicinity of Ethan's lips or fabulous tummy.

'Not bad, but that's why you're the guy who owns the restaurants and I'm lucky enough to eat in them and write about the food.'

He smiled, pointed at her notebook. 'Go ahead, then. Tell me all about the wonders of the seekh kebab.'

She glanced at her notes, a thrill of excitement shooting through her. She loved her job, every amazing moment of it, from sampling food, savouring it, titillating her taste buds until she couldn't put pen to paper fast enough to expound its joys, to trying new concoctions and sharing hidden delights with fellow food addicts.

As for Indian food, she'd been raised on the stuff and there was nothing like it in the world.

'The keema—' he raised an eyebrow and she clarified '—lamb mince is subtly spiced with an exotic blend of garam masala, dried mango powder, carom seeds, raw papaya paste, with a healthy dose of onion, black pepper, ginger, garlic and a pinch of nutmeg.'

'You got all that from one bite?'

She bit her lip as she pushed the notebook away, unable to contain her laughter as he took another bite, trying to figure out how she did it.

'My mum used to make them. I memorised the ingredients when I was ten years old.'

Her laughter petered out as she remembered what else had happened when she was ten—her dad had dropped dead at work, a cerebral aneurysm, and the world as she'd known it had ceased to exist.

She'd loved listening to her parents chat over dinner, their tales of adventure, the story of how they'd met. She'd always craved a once-in-a-lifetime romance like theirs. Richard hadn't been it. Now she'd never find it.

'Hey, you okay?'

She nodded, bit down hard on her bottom lip to stop it quivering. 'I still miss my mum.'

He hesitated before covering her hand with his. 'Tell me about her.'

Tell him what?

How her mum used to braid her waist-length hair into plaits every day for school, never once snagging the brush or rushing her?

How she'd concocted an Indian feast out of rice, lentils, a few spices and little else?

How she'd loved her, protected her, been there for her in every way after her dad had died?

She couldn't put half of what she was feeling into words let alone articulate the devastating sadness reaching down to her barren soul that she was here on this train and Khushi wasn't.

Besides, did she really want to discuss her private memories with him? Revealing her innermost thoughts implied trust and that was one thing she had in short supply, especially with a guy hell-bent on charming her.

'Tell me one of the favourite things you used to do together.'

'Watch Bollywood films,' she said on a sigh, reluctant to talk but surprised by his deeper, caring side, a side too tempting to ignore.

The memory alleviated some of the sadness permeating her thoughts as she remembered many a Sunday afternoon curled up on the worn suede couch in the family room, a plate of jalebis, milk burfi and Mysore pak—delicious Indian sweets made with loads of sugar, milk and butter—between them, as they were riveted to the latest Shah Rukh Khan blockbuster—India's equivalent to Hollywood's top A-list celebrity.

They'd laugh at the over-the-top theatrics, sigh at the vivid romance and natter about the beautiful, vibrant saris.

Raised in Melbourne with an Aussie dad, she'd never felt a huge connection to India, even though her mum's Goan blood flowed in her veins. But for those precious Sunday afternoons she'd been transported to another world—a world filled with people and colour and magic.

'What else?'

'We loved going to the beach.'

His encouragement had her wanting to talk about memories she'd long submerged, memories she only resurrected in the privacy of her room at night when she'd occasionally cry herself to sleep.

Richard's sympathy had been short-lived. He'd told her to get over her grief and focus on more important things, like hosting yet another dinner party for his friends.

That had been three years ago, three long years as their marriage had continued its downward spiral, as her famous husband had slowly revealed a cruel side that, to this day, left her questioning her own judgement in marrying someone like that in the first place.

He'd never actually hit her but the verbal and psychological abuse had been as bruising, as painful, as devastating
as if he had.

Ethan must've sensed her withdrawal, for he continued
prodding. 'Any particular beach?'

She shook her head, the corners of her mouth curving
upwards for the first time since she'd started reminiscing
about her mum.

'It wasn't the location as such. Anywhere would do as
long as there was sand and sun and ocean.'

They'd visited most of the beaches along the Great Ocean
Road after her dad had died: Anglesea, Torquay, Lorne,
Apollo Bay. She'd known why. The beach had reminded
Khushi of meeting her dad for the first time, the story she'd
heard so many times.

Her mum had been trying to hold on to precious memories,
maybe recreate them in her head, but whatever the reason
she'd been happy to go along for the ride. They'd made a great
team and she would've given anything for her mum to pop
into the dining car right now with a wide smile on her face
and her hair perched in a plain bun on top of her head.

'Sounds great.'

'It's why I'm spending a week in Goa after the train. It was
to be the highlight of our trip.'

She took a sip of water, cleared her throat of emotion. 'My
folks met on Colva Beach. Dad was an Aussie backpacker
taking a year off after med school. Mum was working for one
of the hotels there.'

She sighed, swirled the water in her glass. 'Love at first
sight, apparently. My dad used to call Mum his exotic princess
from the Far East, Mum used to say Dad was full of it.'

'Why didn't she ever go back? After he passed away?'

Shrugging, she toyed with her cutlery, the familiar guilt
gnawing at her. 'Because of me, I guess. She wanted me to

have every opportunity education-wise, wanted to raise me as an Australian, as my dad would've wanted.'

'But you're half Indian too. This country is a part of who you are.'

'Honestly? I don't know who I am any more.'

The admission sounded as lost, as forlorn, as she felt almost every minute of every day.

She'd vocalised her greatest fear.

She didn't know who she was, had lost her identity when she'd married Richard. She'd been playing a role for ever: first the dutiful wife, then the grieving widow. But it was all an act. All of it.

She'd become like him, had cared about appearances even at the end when she'd been screaming inside at the injustice of being abused and lied to and cheated on for so long while shedding the appropriate tears at his funeral.

Ethan stood, came around to her side of the table and crouched down, sliding his arm around her waist while tilting her chin to make her look him in the eye with his other hand.

'I know who you are. You're an incredible woman with the world at her feet.' He brushed her cheek in a gentle caress that had tears seeping out of the corners of her eyes. 'Don't you ever, ever forget how truly amazing you are.'

With emotion clogging her throat and tears blinding her, she couldn't speak let alone see what was coming next so when his lips brushed hers in a soft, tender kiss she didn't have time to think, didn't have time to react.

Instead, her eyelids fluttered shut, her aching heart healed just a little as her soul blossomed with wonder at having a man like Ethan Brooks on her side.

His kiss lingered long after he pulled away, long after he stared at her for an interminable moment with shock in the indigo depths of his eyes, long after he murmured the words, 'You're special, that's who you are.'

A small part of her wanted to believe him.

A larger part wanted to recreate the magic of that all-too-brief kiss, as for the second time in a week she felt like a woman.

The largest part of her recoiled in horror as she realised she'd just been kissed—again—by the last man she could get close to, ever.

Ethan sprang to his feet and catapulted back to his chair on the opposite side of the table, desperate for space.

She'd done it again.

Left him reeling with her power to undermine his control.

Those damn tears had done it, tugging at nonexistent heart-strings, urging him to kiss her, to comfort her, making him *feel,* damn it.

He'd been a fool, urging her to talk about her mum. He should've known she'd get emotional, should've figured he'd want to play the hero and help slay her demons.

'You're good at that.'

His gaze snapped to hers, expecting wariness, thrown by her curiosity, as if she couldn't quite figure him out.

'At what?'

'Knowing when to say the right thing, knowing how to make a girl feel good about herself.'

'Practice, I guess.'

If his offhand shrug hadn't made her recoil, his callous comment did the trick.

He'd just lumped her in with the rest of his conquests—something she'd hate, something he hated.

But it had to be done.

He needed distance right now, needed to slam his emotional barriers back in place and muster the control troops to the battlefront.

'Lucky me.'

Her sarcasm didn't sock him half as much as her expression, a potent mix of disappointment and derision.

He had to take control of this situation before it got out of hand and he ended up alienating her completely, and all because he was furious at himself for getting too close.

'Before I put you off your food with any more of my renowned comforting techniques, why don't we finish off this entrée? I've heard the lentil curry to come is something special.'

She nodded, her disappointment slugging him anew as she toyed with the food on her plate.

Establishing emotional distance was paramount. He'd come close to losing sight of his seduction goal moments before but steeling his heart was one thing, carrying it through with a disillusioned Tam sitting opposite another.

'What do you think of the potato bondas?'

An innocuous question, a question designed to distract her from his abrupt turnaround and get them back on the road of comfortable small talk.

However, as she raised her gaze from her plate and met his, the accusatory hurt reached down to his soul, as if he were the worst kind of louse.

For a moment he thought she'd call him on his brusque switch from comforting to cool. Instead, she searched his face, her mouth tightening as if what she saw confirmed her worst opinion of him.

'They're good.'

Hating feeling out of his depth, he pushed the platter towards her. 'Another?'

'No, thanks.'

They lapsed into silence, an awkward silence fraught with unspoken words—words he couldn't bring himself to say for fear of the growing intimacy between them.

Being here with her wasn't about establishing an emotional connection, it was about seducing the one woman he'd wanted for years and couldn't have.

He needed to keep it that way, for the other option scared the life out of him.

CHAPTER FOUR

ETHAN focused on the tour guide as he droned on about Hawa Mahal, the Palace of the Winds.

Structurally, the place was amazing, like a giant candy-floss beehive with its tiers of windows staggered in red and pink sandstone.

Architecture usually fascinated him—every restaurant he purchased around the world was chosen for position as well as aesthetics—but, while the guide pointed out the white borders and motifs of Jaipur's multi-layered palace, he sneaked glances at the woman standing next to him, apparently engrossed in what the guy had to say. While he, Ethan, was engrossed in her.

As the train had wound its way from New Delhi to the 'Pink City' of Jaipur overnight, he'd lain awake, hands clasped behind his head, staring at the ceiling.

For hours. Long, endless hours, replaying that comfy scene over dinner and cursing himself for being a fool.

He'd overstepped with the cosy chat about her mum, had panicked and back-pedalled as a result.

The upshot? Tam's barriers had slammed down, shutting him out, obliterating what little ground he'd made since she'd forgiven him for crashing her trip.

Stupid, stupid, stupid.

Ever since he'd boarded the train he'd been edgy, unfocused, displaced. And he hated feeling like that, as if he had no control.

Everyone said he was a control freak and, to some degree, he was. Control gave him power and impenetrability and confidence that things would work out exactly as he planned them, at total odds with his childhood, where no amount of forethought could give him the stability he'd so desperately craved.

When he'd first landed in this cosmopolitan, jam-packed country, he'd had a clear goal: to seduce Tam.

He wanted her—had always wanted her—but had stayed away for business reasons. Richard had been the best chef in the country and he'd needed him to cement Ambrosia's reputation.

Nothing got in his way when his most prized possession was at stake, not even a beautiful, intelligent woman. He hadn't needed the distraction at the time, had been hell-bent on making Ambrosia Melbourne's premier dining experience.

He'd succeeded, thanks to Richard's flamboyance in the kitchen and a healthy dose of business acumen on his part. Now, nothing stood in his way. Discounting his stupid overeagerness, that was.

He sneaked another sideways glance at Tam, wondering if her intent focus was genuine or another way to give him the cold shoulder.

She wasn't like the other women he'd dated: everything, from her reluctance to respond to his flirting to the lingering sadness in her eyes, told him she wouldn't take kindly to being wooed.

He hoped to change all that.

'Some structure, huh?'

She finally turned towards him, her expression cool, her eyes wary.

'Yeah, it's impressive.' She pointed at one of the windows. 'Don't you think it's amazing all those royal women of the palace used to sit behind those windows and watch the ceremonial processions without being seen?'

He squinted, saw a pink window like a hundred others and shook his head.

'Sad, more like it. Having to stay behind closed doors while the kings got to strut their stuff. Don't think many women would put up with that these days.'

She stiffened, hurt flickering in the rich green depths of her eyes.

'Maybe some women find it's easier to give in to the whims of their husbands than live with callous coldness every day.'

Realisation dawned and he thrust his hands in his pockets to stop from slapping himself in the head. Had she just inadvertently given him a glimpse into her marriage to Richard?

He'd seen Rich like that at work. All smiles and jovial conviviality but if things didn't go his way or someone dared to have a different opinion to King Dick, he'd freeze them out better than his Bombe Alaska.

Would he have ever treated his wife the same way?

He hated thinking that this warm, vibrant woman had been subjected to that, had possibly tiptoed around in order to stay on his good side, had put a happy face on a marriage that would've been trying at best.

She didn't deserve that, no woman did, and the least he could do now was distract her long enough so she forgot his unintentional faux pas and enjoyed the rest of their day in Jaipur.

'I've seen enough palaces for one day. How about you and I hit some of those handicraft shops the guide mentioned earlier?' He bent towards her ear, spoke in an exaggerated conspiratorial whisper. 'By your different footwear for breakfast, lunch and dinner, I'd say you collect shoes on a weekly basis so I'm sure the odd bargain or two wouldn't go astray.'

She straightened her shoulders, flashed him a superior

smirk while her eyes sparkled. 'I'll have you know I only buy a few pairs of shoes a year, mainly boots. Melbourne's winters can be a killer on a girl's feet.'

'I'll take your word for it.'

He smiled, thrilled that his distraction technique had worked when she returned it. 'So, you up for some shopping?'

'I'm up for anything.'

Their gazes locked and for a long, loaded moment he could've sworn he saw a flicker of something other than her usual reticence.

'Come on then, let's go.'

As she fell in step beside him, his mind mulled over her revelation. He had no idea what sort of a marriage Rich and Tam had shared; he'd barely seen them together, preferring to make himself scarce whenever she'd appeared.

He'd cited interstate or overseas business whenever she'd hosted a party and had avoided all contact if she dropped into Ambrosia to see Rich on the odd occasion.

In fact, he'd rarely seen the two interact, such had been his blinding need to avoid her at all costs.

Maybe he was reading too much into her comment about tolerant wives and their private battle to keep the peace? Probably a passing comment, nothing more.

Then why the persistent nagging that maybe there was more behind her fragility than ongoing grief for a dead husband?

Jamming his hands into his pockets, he picked up the pace. The sooner they hit the shops, the sooner she'd be distracted and the sooner he'd lose the urge to bundle her in his arms, cradle her close and murmur soothing words again. Last night had been bad enough and he had no intention of treading down that road again.

He shouldn't get involved.

Her marriage was her business and the less he thought about it the better. Remembering she had once loved another man enough to marry him didn't sit real well considering how much he wanted her.

Besides, it would be dangerous—very dangerous—for Tam to become emotionally attached to him and that was exactly what would happen if he started delving into issues that didn't concern him and offering comfort.

He didn't do emotions, hated the wild, careening, out-of-control feelings they produced, which was why he dated widely and frequently and never got involved.

Never.

Better off sticking to what he knew best: work. He understood work. He could control work. He could become the man he'd always wanted to be through work. That suited him just fine.

As for Tam, he'd concentrate on keeping things light and sticking to his original plan.

These days, what he wanted he got and he had his sights firmly fixed on her.

She was no good at this.

Her plan to freeze Ethan out had hit a snag. A big one, in the shape of one super-smooth, super-charming, super-likeable pain in the butt.

She wanted to maintain a polite distance between them to ensure he didn't get the wrong idea—that she was actually starting to enjoy his flirting.

A long camel ride across the sand dunes of Jaiselmar had been perfect for her plan. Little opportunity for conversation, lots of concentration required to stay on the loping dromedaries.

But she hadn't counted on arriving at this romantic haven in the middle of the desert for an early dinner, nor had she counted on the persistent attention of one determined guy.

She'd been so close to seriously liking him last night, when he'd encouraged her to talk about her mum. To trust him enough to do that alarmed her, for it meant she was falling under his legendary spell.

Thankfully, he'd retreated quicker than she had at the sound of Richard's footfall after work and, while she'd been hurt at the time, she was now grateful.

Smooth, charming Ethan she could handle—just.

Caring, compassionate Ethan had the power to undo her completely.

So she'd retreated too, limiting their time spent together by taking breakfast in her carriage rather than the dining car, making boring, polite small talk at lunch.

Now, forced to be in his company on this tour, she'd maintained her freeze but, despite her monosyllabic responses, her deliberate long silences and her focused attention on the horizon, he persisted.

For some reason, Ethan was determined to get her to respond to him as a man. Why? Why here, why now?

They'd crossed paths infrequently over the last year and he'd been nothing but super-professional, almost aloof. So what was with the charming act?

He'd gone from teasing to full-on flirting and, try as she might, she couldn't maintain her freeze much longer. Under the scorching Indian sun, there was a serious thaw coming.

'Pretty spectacular, huh?'

With a weary sigh, she turned to face him, instantly wishing she hadn't when that piercing blue-eyed gaze fixed on her with purpose.

'Sure is.'

Her gaze drifted back to the beautiful tent city silhouetted against a setting sun, the sky an entrancing combination of indigo streaked with mauve and magenta where it dipped to the horizon, a sweep of golden sands as far as she could see.

A tingle rippled through her and she shivered, captivated by the beauty of a land she felt more for with each passing day.

This was why she'd come—to reconnect with herself, with her past. When she'd first booked this trip she'd envisioned shedding tears, letting go of some of her anger and discovering that missing part of herself tied up in this mystical country.

Never in her wildest dreams had she anticipated feeling like this. Not that she could verbalise what *this* was.

But every time Ethan had glanced at her she felt overwhelmed, dizzy, off-kilter, *alive.*

It was more than his inherent ability to coax a smile to her face, to make her laugh despite the unrelenting bitterness weaving a constricting net around her heart

No, there was more—much more than she could handle. An off-guard glance, a loaded stare, a little current of something arcing between them like the faintest invisible thread—intangible, insubstantial, yet there all the same.

And it terrified her.

This journey had been about self-discovery. Well, she'd certainly discovered more about herself than she'd anticipated in the startling, frightening fact that she was attracted to a man totally wrong for her.

'Let's get something to eat.'

She forced herself to relax as Ethan helped her down from the camel by holding her hand and placing his other in the small of her back, a small gesture which meant nothing.

So why the heat from his palm through her thin cotton sundress, the little tingle skittering along her skin, making her wish he'd linger?

She could blame this new awareness on India, its wild, untamed edge bringing out the same in her. But she'd be lying, and if there was one thing she'd learned through her fiasco of a marriage it was never to lie to herself again.

As he held open a tent flap for her and gestured for her to enter, his enquiring gaze locked onto hers and she swallowed at the desire she glimpsed.

He knew she was trying to avoid him and he didn't care.

So much passed in that one loaded stare: challenge, intent and heat—loads of heat that sizzled and zapped and had her diving into the tent for a reprieve.

She was crazy. Playing it cool with Ethan had been a monumental error in judgement. A guy like him would now see her as a challenge and she'd be darned if she sat back and watched him try to charm his way into her good graces. She wasn't interested in anything remotely romantic and, even if she was, he'd be the last guy she'd turn to.

'You can't keep up the silent treatment for ever.'

The amusement in his voice only served to irk more.

'Watch me.'

She swivelled on her heel and he grabbed her arm, leaving her no option but to face him while trying to ignore the erratic leap of her pulse at his innocuous touch.

'So I kissed you again? It was nothing. Surely we can get past it?'

Ouch, that hurt.

Of course a kiss would mean nothing to a playboy like him and, while she should be glad he was brushing it off, a small part of her hurt. She'd done her best to forget it, but she couldn't.

The kiss last night had been different from the impulsive, passionate kiss in Ambrosia the day he'd returned.

This kiss had been filled with tenderness and compassion and understanding, his gentle consideration in stark contrast to the powerful man she knew him to be and thus so much more appealing.

This kiss had unlocked something deep inside, the touch of his lips bringing to life a part of her assumed long dead.

That something was hope.

'Come on, Tam. What do you say we put it behind us and enjoy this lovely spread?'

He waved towards the linen-covered tables covered in a

staggering array of mouth-watering dishes she normally would've pounced on if her stomach wasn't tied in knots, the hint of that pirate smile tugging at his mouth.

How could a woman resist?

'Okay. But, just so you know, I'm not interested in anything…er…what I mean to say is…'

'It was just a kiss.' He ducked down to murmur in her ear and she gritted her teeth as a surge of renewed lust burst through her at his warm breath fanning her cheek. 'An all too short one at that.'

'I've heard that one before.'

'About it being just a kiss? Or me not apologising for it?'

'Yeah, that. It's a catchphrase of yours.'

He laughed, released her arm, and headed for the table, leaving her torn between wanting to shake him and admiring him for not backing down.

She sank into the chair he held out for her as a waiter bearing several silver-domed platters bore down on their table, deposited their meal, whipped off the domes and retreated with a small bow.

The fragrant aromas of spicy curries never failed to set her salivating but tonight her stomach clenched as she realized, no matter what she said to him, he'd continue to do exactly what he liked—and that was flirt with her.

'I'd like to propose a toast.'

He picked up his champagne flute, waited for her to do the same.

'To new beginnings and new experiences. May this journey bring us everything we could possibly wish for.'

Tam stared into her flute, watching the effervescent bubbles float lazily to the surface.

New beginnings, new experiences…hadn't she wanted all that and more on this trip? So why was she getting hot and bothered over a little harmless flirtation?

She knew Ethan's reputation, that flirting would come as easily as his millions. It meant nothing to him, he'd said so. She was so out of practice dealing with a charming man she'd lost perspective. Time to chill out.

'To new beginnings.'

She lifted her glass, tapped his, before raising it to her lips, wondering if the slight buzz was from the bubbles sliding down her throat or his mischievous smile.

'Let's eat.'

Silence reigned as they tucked into Jaipuri Mewa Pulao, a spiced rice packed with dried fruit, Rajasthani Lal Maas, a deliciously spiced lamb and Aloo Bharta, potato with a chilli kick, with relish.

As each new flavour burst on her tongue the words to describe them flashed through her mind in the way they'd always done when she'd worked full-time, vindication that the time was right to get back to the workforce on her return. Rather than being nervous, she couldn't wait.

As Ethan licked his lips and moaned with pleasure, she laughed. 'I take it you're enjoying Rajasthani cuisine.'

'Can't get enough of it.'

Popping another ladle of potato onto his plate, he nodded. 'Want to hear a fascinating fact I heard from our tour leader?'

'Uh-huh.'

'Rajasthan is an ancient princely state and it gave rise to a royal cuisine. The Rajas would go on hunting expeditions and eat the meat or fowl they brought back, which is why their feasts flaunt meat.'

'It all sounds very cavemanish.'

He glanced around, as if searching for something. 'Where's my club?' Accompanied by a ludicrous wiggle of his eyebrows. 'Fancy checking out my cave?'

She chuckled, glad she'd made the decision to lighten up. Sharing a meal with a charismatic dinner companion was enjoyable and definitely more fun than dining alone, something she'd honed to a fine art in the last year.

Though, in reality, she'd been alone a lot longer than that, Richard's long absences put down to work or media appearances or travelling to promote his latest book. Oh, not forgetting the time he'd spent holed away with his mistress.

Before she could mull further, he shot her a concerned glance and pushed the platter of potato towards her. 'More?'

Grateful for his distracting ploy, she nodded and ladled more food onto her plate.

'How did you get your start as a food critic?'

Another distraction and she silently applauded his ability to read her moods. Though it wouldn't take a genius to figure out her expression must've soured at the thought of Richard and his girlfriend.

'I've always been passionate about food and I loved telling a good story at school. So I worked in a professional kitchen for a while, cultivated my palate outside of it, immersed myself in all things food, then spent a year as a hostess at Pulse.'

'You must've learned a lot there. That place was big—before Ambrosia opened, of course.'

She smiled. 'Of course.'

She'd loved her experience in the industry: being able to give an in-depth description of an entire meal, the restaurant, its décor, how the service contributed to the dining experience. Work had never been a chore for her and, thanks to Ethan and the opportunity he'd given her at Ambrosia for the last six months, she now had the confidence to get back to it.

'Can I ask you a stupid question?'

'Sure.'

'Does all that writing spoil the fun of eating for you?'

She shook her head. 'Uh-uh. I love to eat, I love what I do. It's as simple as that.'

And as they made desultory small talk over dessert,

Churma Laddoos—sweet balls made from flour, ghee, sugar, almonds and cardamoms—she pondered her words.

As simple as that.

Were things simple and she was complicating them?

She'd wanted to expand her mindset on this trip, wanted to explore a side of her long quashed, away from the sour memories dogging her, away from Richard's malevolent presence still hanging over her.

While she had no interest in romance, maybe she could explore the side of her long ignored?

She was a woman—a woman who'd had her self-esteem battered severely, to the point where she didn't trust her judgement any more.

Maybe Ethan could help reaffirm the woman she'd once been—a woman who'd loved to smile and laugh and flirt right back.

She longed to be that woman again.

But would she have the courage to try?

CHAPTER FIVE

'IT'S beautiful.'

They stood inside Udaipur's Jag Niwas, the stunning Lake Palace that rose out of the blue waters of Lake Pichhola like an incredible apparition, looking out over the rippling, murmuring waves lapping the foreshore.

When Tamara had been planning this trip with her mum, she'd wanted to stay in this dreamlike marble palace with its ornately carved columns and tinkling fountains and clouds of chiffon drapes, now a grand heritage hotel.

Now, with Ethan by her side, she was glad she wasn't. The last thing she needed was to stay in some exquisitely romantic hotel with a man putting unwanted romantic ideas into her head.

She turned away from the picture-perfect view, gestured to the silver-laden table behind them. 'You ready to eat?'

He nodded, dropped his hand, and she clamped down on the instant surge of disappointment. 'Business all done. The chef signed the contract in front of me.'

He pulled out her chair in a characteristic chivalrous act she loved. If Richard had ever done it, he'd plonked his own selfish ass in it before she could move.

'He's one of India's best. And, considering my other choice in Delhi wouldn't budge, it's a coup getting this guy on board. Can't wait for him to start at Ambrosia.'

She sat, smiled her thanks. 'If you can't wait, neither can I. Just think, I get to sample his Chicken Makhani and crab curry and sweet potato kheer for nothing, all in the name of work.'

He chuckled, sat opposite her and flicked out his pristine white linen napkin like a troubadour before laying it in his lap.

'It's a hard life but somebody's got to do it, right?'

'Right.'

Hope cradled her heart, warming it, melting the band of anguish circling it. This was one of those moments she'd grown to crave yet fear, a poignant moment filled with closeness and intimacy.

A moment that said she was a fool for thinking she could start testing her flirting prowess and come out unscathed— or, worse, wanting more.

He broke the spell by picking up the menu, scanning it. 'Let me guess. You've already studied this in great depth and have your trusty notebook at the ready.'

She tossed her hair over her shoulder, sent him a snooty stare that lost some of its impact when her lips twitched.

'My trusty notebook is safe in my bag.'

He raised an eyebrow and sent a pointed look at her favourite patent black handbag hanging off the back of her chair.

'No notes today?'

'Not a one.'

The corners of his mouth kicked up into the deliciously gorgeous smile that had launched this crazy new awareness in the first place. 'Well, well, maybe you're starting to like my company after all.'

'Maybe.'

She picked up a menu, ducked behind it to hide a faint blush.

'Want to know what I think?'

He leaned forward, beckoned her with a crook of a finger, leaving her no option but to do it.

'You're going to tell me anyway, so go ahead.'

He murmured behind his hand, 'I think that notebook is like Bankie.'

'Bankie?'

'The security blanket I had when I was a toddler. I couldn't say blanket, so called it Bankie. A frayed, worn, faded blue thing that went everywhere I did.'

Her heart turned over, imagining how utterly adorable he would've looked as a wide-eyed two-year-old clinging to his blanket.

He'd never spoken of his family but she assumed he had one tucked away somewhere; probably parents who doted on their wonder-boy son and a proud sibling or two.

'Why do you think I need a security blanket?'

'Because of what's happening between us.'

Her belly plummeted. She didn't want to have this conversation, not here, not now, not ever.

Darn it, until now she could've dismissed the awareness between them as a figment of her imagination.

Now it was out there.

Between them.

Larger than life and more terrifying than anything she could've possibly imagined.

She could ignore it, try and bluff her way out of it. But this was Ethan. The guy who'd helped her with the legal rigmarole after Richard's funeral, the guy who'd given her a chance at getting her career back on track. She owed him her thanks if not the truth.

'Seeing as you keep kissing me, what do you think is happening between us?'

He paused, shifted his plate and cutlery around before intertwining his fingers and laying his hands on the table and leaning forward.

'Honestly? I like you.'

He leaned closer, lowered his voice, and she had no option

but to lean closer too. 'I like that you've changed since we've arrived here.'

This she could handle. She could fob him off with the real reason behind her change: her journey of self-discovery, her awakening to being her own person, her enjoyment of answering to no one but herself. All perfectly legitimate reasons to satisfy his curiosity and hide the real reason behind her change.

She shrugged, aiming for nonchalance. 'India's in my blood. Maybe my inner self recognises it on some subconscious level.'

He shook his head. 'I think there's more to it.'

'Like?'

'Like you opening your mind. Like you contemplating maybe there could be a spark between us.'

'I'm not contemplating anything of the sort!'

It sounded like the big fat lie it was.

He merely smiled, a captivating, sexy smile that made her feel a woman and then some.

'Come on, Tam. Admit it. You're as attracted to me as I am to you.'

She pushed away from the table, stood abruptly. 'I'm going for a walk.'

He let her go but she knew it wouldn't be for long. While he'd been surprisingly relaxed and laid-back on this trip, she'd seen his underlying streak of steel that had taken him to the top of the restaurant game around the world.

He'd made every rich list the year before, had women clamouring after him. So what the heck was he doing harassing a boring, sad-case widow like her?

She headed for the lake, head down, sandals flapping against the ancient stone path, eager to be anywhere other than sitting opposite the man she *was* attracted to in a palace restaurant in one of the most romantic settings on earth.

'Hey, wait up.'

His shout had her wanting to pick up the pace and flee. Futile, really, because she'd be stuck on the train with him for another few nights regardless if she outran him now.

Slowing her steps, she reached the edge of the lake, staring into the endless depths, searching for some clue to her problem, the problem of opening her heart to trust again, only to find the guy she liked was the one most likely to break it.

She knew when he reached her, could sense his body heat behind her, and she turned slowly, no closer to answering him now than she had been a few moments earlier.

He reached for her, dropped his hands when she frowned.

'You know I'm blunt. I call it as I see it and, deny it all you like, but something's happening between us.'

'Nothing's happening.'

A sudden breeze snatched her defiant whisper, making a mockery of her feeble protestation.

'If that's what you want to believe…' He shrugged, turned away, stared out over the lake to the island in the middle housing an entertainment complex where they'd have afternoon tea later, giving her time to concoct more excuses, more repudiation.

As if time would help.

She could protest all she liked but it wouldn't change the fact that everything had shifted and she didn't have a clue what to do about it.

How could she tell him that acknowledging the attraction between them, let alone giving in to it, was beyond frightening? How could she make him understand what a big deal this was for her?

It came to her as she glanced at his profile: so rugged, so handsome, so strong. She needed his strength, needed someone in her corner.

She'd never felt so alone as this last year, the last few years, despite being married and the implicit promise of safety it provided. And, while Ethan was the last guy she'd turn to for safety, having him here, every enigmatic, enthralling, enticing inch of him, being more honest than Richard had ever been, went a long way to soothing her fear that this crazy, burgeoning physical need for him was totally wrong.

She laid a hand on his arm, dropped it when he turned towards her.

'Want to know what I believe? I believe you're a good guy. You make me laugh when you tell those horrible corny jokes. You make me smile with your outrageous flirting. But, most of all, you've made me believe I can have a fresh start.'

Some nebulous emotion bordering on guilt shifted in his eyes before he blinked. 'Good guy? Far from it.'

He glanced away, rubbed the back of his neck. 'I think you're amazing and I'm attracted to you, but don't go thinking I'm some prince because I'm not.'

'I gave up expecting a prince to rescue me a long time ago,' she said, annoyed she'd let slip another indication that Richard had been anything other than the guy Ethan thought him to be.

He searched her face—for answers, for the truth?

'You want me to drop this? Pretend it doesn't exist?'

That was exactly what she wanted but, for one tiny moment, the faintest hope in her heart that there could ever be anything more between them snuffed out like a candle in the breeze.

'Yes,' she breathed on a sigh, wishing there could be another way, knowing there wasn't.

She'd lost her mother, her husband and her identity over the last few years and she'd be darned if she lost the chance at a new start.

Falling for Ethan would be beyond foolish, destined to shatter what little of her trust remained and there was no way she'd put herself through something like that ever again.

A new hardness turned his eyes to steely blue as he nodded. 'Fine, have it your way. But know this. Pretending something doesn't exist won't make it disappear.'

He turned on his heel and strode towards the palace, leaving her heart heaving and her soul reaching out an imaginary hand to him, grasping, desperate, before falling uselessly to her side.

He wouldn't give up.

It was a motto that had got him through a horror childhood, the nightmare of his teens, and had taken him to the top of the restaurateur game.

Right now, what was at stake was just as important as scavenging for the next food scrap to fill his howling belly or opening a new restaurant in New York.

Tam had blossomed, had become a woman who smiled and laughed and raised her face to a scorching Indian sun. She ran through ancient forts. She sampled the spiciest dishes and called for more chilli. She played with the little children who dogged their steps when the train stopped, bestowing smiles and hugs and her last rupees.

This was the woman he wanted with an unrelenting fierceness that constantly tore at him, an overwhelming need out of proportion to anything he'd remotely felt before.

Now she'd let down her guard, was attracted to him. He could see it in the newly sparkling eyes, the quick look-away when he captured her gaze, the smile never far from her lips, which had been constantly downturned until recently.

And, no matter how much she wanted to pretend, this attraction wasn't going away. Not if he had anything to do with it.

In the business arena, he was notorious for his ruthlessness, his take-charge and take-no-prisoners attitude. He didn't have much time left with Tam and, the way he saw it, he needed to make something happen—now.

He just hoped she'd still talk to him after she discovered what he'd done to help them along a little.

She stood at the bow of the boat, a vision in a white dress scattered with vivid pink and red flowers, her hair loose and flowing around her shoulders, fluttering in the breeze.

He'd never seen anything so beautiful, so vibrant, so stunning, and his desire for her slammed into him anew.

Yeah, he was through waiting. He'd waited years already and now there was nothing standing in his way.

She glanced up at that exact moment, sending him a tentative smile, and he strode towards her, needing little invitation to be right by her side.

'You sure we've got time to cruise the lake and check out the entertainment complex on the island?'

He glanced at his watch, noting the time with satisfaction. 'Plenty of time.'

The glib lie slid from his lips and he didn't regret it, not for a second.

Udaipur's Lake Palace was one of the most romantic hotels on earth and if he couldn't convince her to confront their attraction here, it wouldn't happen anywhere.

She smiled and he instantly quashed his yearning to slip a possessive arm around her waist as his heart slammed against his rib cage and his blood thickened with the drugging desire to make her his.

'You sure? We wouldn't want to miss the train and be stuck in this place.'

She waved towards the tranquil lake, the Palace on the far shore. 'I mean, staying in the hotel wouldn't be a hardship, but stuck with you? Now, that'd be tough.'

Ignoring the flicker of guilt that he was instigating just such an outcome, he propped his elbows on the railing and leaned back.

'Are you actually teasing me?'

She glanced at him from beneath lowered lashes and he could've punched the air with elation that she was lightening up enough to spar with him.

'Maybe.'

'Well, if this is the reaction I get for suggesting a simple boat ride, I'm going to do it more often.'

The light in her eyes faded as her gaze left his to sweep the horizon.

'I'll be busy relaunching my career when we get back to Melbourne and you'll be too busy being the hotshot businessman so I think any boat rides down the Yarra are wishful thinking.'

Was that her way of saying what happened in India stayed in India? That, even if she eventually capitulated and acknowledged their attraction or, as he was hoping, did something about it, things would come to an abrupt end when they got home?

'In that case, let's make the most of our time cruising here.'

'Okay.'

He didn't push the issue and it earned him a grateful glance, but he didn't want her gratitude, damn it. He wanted her to look at him with stars in her eyes and hope in her heart—hope that they could be more than friends.

'Speaking of Melbourne, can I ask you a question?'

She could ask him to take a flying leap and he'd ask how high. 'Sure, shoot.'

'You and Richard were mates. Why didn't I see you at the dinner parties he was so fond of? And, when we did cross paths, it was almost like you avoided me.'

Her question hit too close to home and dread settled like overcooked Beef Wellington in the pit of his stomach, solid and heavy with discomfort assured.

Since he'd started pursuing her he'd known they'd have this

conversation one day, surprised it'd taken her this long to ask and wishing it wasn't here, now, when he was making serious headway in his quest to have her.

'I wasn't avoiding you.'

'No?'

What could he say?

That he'd wanted her so badly he'd kept his distance for fear it'd distract him from his job? Or, worse, cause a serious problem between him and Rich, thus affecting their business?

That he'd wanted her so badly he'd dated a few look-alikes?

That he'd been so envious of Rich he'd taken a month off from the restaurant when they'd married?

That he'd been unable to look at the two of them together without wanting to hit something in frustration?

'I guess we moved in the same social circles occasionally, but I was busy schmoozing or courting business deals at those events to make chit-chat. Business, you know how it is.'

He avoided her shrewd stare by looking over her shoulder at the Palace shimmering in the distance. 'Never enough hours in the day.'

'Yet, by all accounts, you have plenty of time to date. Hmm…'

She tapped her bottom lip, drawing his attention to its fullness; as if he needed reminding. 'I guess what the rumour mill says about you is true.'

'What's that?'

'You're a seasoned playboy and Melbourne's number one eligible bachelor.'

'Playboy, huh?'

Her teasing smile surprised him, warming him better than the fiery vindaloo he'd sampled at lunch. 'Bet you're proud of it too.'

He pretended to ponder for all of a second before shrugging, feigning bashfulness.

'That's some title. Care to help me live up to my reputation?'

He expected her to leap overboard at what he was suggesting but once again she surprised him, merely quirking an eyebrow, her smile widening.

'What? And become yet another statistic?' She shook her head. 'Nope, sorry, no can do. But don't worry, I'm sure you'll have loads of dewy-eyed, stick insect bimbos lining up when your plane touches down at Tullamarine.'

He chuckled, only slightly disconcerted by the fact that she'd described his usual dates to a T.

'Are you implying I'm shallow, Miss Rayne?'

'I'm not implying anything. I'm stating a fact.'

She joined in his laughter and he marvelled at the transformation from reserved widow to relaxed woman. He'd always thought her beautiful but when she was like this— laughing, laissez-faire—she was simply stunning.

'Lucky for you, the boat's about to dock. I don't think my ego could take much more of your kid-glove treatment.'

'There's plenty more where that came from.'

'I stand duly warned.'

As they disembarked, Ethan didn't have a care in the world. The woman he wanted was definitely warming to him and they'd have several days together away from the train to get to know each other much better.

He was making things happen, was back in control— exactly where he wanted to be.

'What do you mean, we missed the train?'

Tamara stared at Ethan in open-mouthed shock, his calm expression only serving to wind her up. 'You said we had plenty of time.'

He shrugged, checked his watch again. 'I made a mistake. Sorry.'

'*Sorry?* Is that all you can say?'

As the concierge glanced their way, she lowered her voice with effort. 'This is ridiculous.'

'Look, it's no big deal. We get a couple of rooms for the night, make arrangements to catch the train at the next stop.'

'It's not that easy.'

She sank into the nearest chair, tired after their long day, annoyed he'd made them miss the train and afraid—terribly afraid—of spending the night in this romantic hotel with Ethan.

There was a difference between not acknowledging the simmering attraction between them, the newly awakened awareness that shimmered between them hotter than the Indian sun, and trying to ignore it in a place like this.

'We'll miss the next stop tomorrow and that leaves the last day, the most important of the whole trip.'

'Because of the Taj?'

She nodded, a tiny pinch of latent grief nipping her heart. 'And the birds. My mum was obsessed with birds. She collected figurines of anything from geese to cranes and she always wanted to visit Bharatpur's bird sanctuary.'

He must've caught the hint of wistfulness mingled with sadness in her tone, for he pulled his mobile out of his pocket and leapt to his feet.

'I'll handle this. We'll stay here tonight and tomorrow we'll head to Bharatpur, then Agra.'

Before she could respond, he was already punching numbers on his phone. 'Don't worry, you won't miss a thing.'

'But all my clothes are on board. I don't have—'

'I'll sort everything out. Trust me.'

He held up a finger as someone answered on the other end and she snuggled into the comfortable lobby sofa, grateful to be stuck with someone so commanding.

She was tired of making decisions over the last year: when to return to work, what to do with the house, with her stock in Ambrosia, to take this trip. Sure, she'd appreciated the independence, especially since she'd been robbed of it for so long, but here, now, with Ethan taking charge, she was happy to sit back and go with the flow.

Strangely, she did trust him—with their travel arrangements, at least. He'd make things happen, he was that kind of guy.

'Right, all taken care of.'

He snapped the phone shut, thrust it into his pocket and dusted off his hands, mission accomplished.

'With one phone call?'

He grinned and held out a hand to help her up from the sofa. 'My PA's handling all the arrangements. In the meantime, let's grab a room.'

Her heart stuttered, her pulse skipped and she broke out in a cold sweat before realising it was just a figure of speech. He meant two rooms; he'd said as much earlier.

'Or we could get the honeymoon suite if you're feeling particularly adventurous.'

Her shocked gaze flew to his, only to find his too-blue eyes twinkling adorably.

With a shake of her head, she waved him away. 'As tempting as that sounds, I've already told you I'm not another statistic.'

His mischievous grin had her wishing she could throw caution to the wind and become just that.

'Too bad, my bedpost needs a new notch.'

'You're—'

'Adorable? Endearing? Growing on you?'

Biting the inside of her cheek to stop herself from laughing out loud, she said, 'Pushing your luck. I'm beat. How about we get a *couple* of rooms?'

She only just caught his muttered, 'Spoilsport,' under his breath as he proceeded to charm the check-in staff as easily as he did everyone else.

Glancing around at the pristine marble floor, the majestic

columns, the sweeping staircase and the glistening chandeliers, she couldn't help but be glad.

She was spending the night in a beautiful palace on a world famous lake with the most charming man she'd ever met.

And while she could vehemently deny her insane attraction to a guy so totally wrong for her, it didn't hurt to let some of the romance of this place soften the edges of her hard resolve. Right?

Oh, boy.

There was a difference between softening her resolve and it melting clean away, and right now, staring at Ethan in her doorway, with champagne in one hand and a glossy Taj brochure in the other, she knew her resolve wasn't softening, it was in tatters.

'Mind if I come in?'

Yeah, she minded, especially since she'd rinsed her dress and underwear and was in a fluffy complimentary hotel robe.

If she felt vulnerable to him in her clothes, what hope did she have naked?

Oh, no, she couldn't think about being naked under her robe, not with him staring at her with those twinkling cobalt eyes, and the mere thought had a blush creeping into her cheeks.

'I come bearing gifts.'

He waved the champagne and brochure to tempt her. As if he wouldn't be enough to do that. The thought had her clutching the door, ready to close it.

'Actually, I'm pretty tired.'

And confused and drained and just a tad excited.

He'd showered too and, with his slicked-back wet hair, persuasive sexy smile and magnetic indigo eyes, he looked more like a pirate than ever.

Ethan was dangerous: too glib, too smooth, too gorgeous.

At that moment, she knew exactly why she found him so

attractive. She'd married Richard because he'd made her feel safe. The older guy who loved her, took care of her, made her feel special, and while it may not have lasted, that hadn't stopped her from cherishing the feeling of security he'd temporarily brought to her life.

Which explained why she suddenly found Ethan so appealing. That edge of danger, of unpredictability, was something she'd never experienced and, while she wouldn't want someone like him in her life, for someone who'd played it safe her entire life, she could understand the allure.

He held up the brochure, cleverly honing in on her weak spot. 'Share one drink with me, whet my appetite for the Taj Mahal and I'm out of here. Promise.'

Her instincts screamed to refuse but he'd been nothing but helpful in organising their rooms, transport for tomorrow and entry to the bird sanctuary and the Taj. The least she could do was appear grateful rather than churlish.

'Okay.'

Besides, it was only one drink. Barely enough time to make small talk, let alone anything else happening. Not that she wanted anything to happen.

Great, there went another blush. She quickly opened the door further and ushered him in.

'Room okay?'

'Are you kidding?'

When she'd wanted to stay here, she'd had no idea the rooms would be this gorgeous: the cusped archways, the carvings, the Bohemian crystal lights and the miniature paintings. It was like living in a fairy tale, being a princess for a night.

As long as there was no pea under the mattress, and no prince on top of it.

'It's fantastic.'

'Good. For a while there, I thought you'd behead me for making us miss the train.'

'Wasn't like you did it on purpose.'

Guilt tightened his features as he turned away to uncork the champagne and pour it into the exquisite crystal flutes which were standard room supplies, but it disappeared as he handed her a glass, joined her on the sofa; she must've imagined it.

'Here's to the rest of the trip being as eventful.'

He raised his glass to hers, tapped it and drank, his eyes never leaving hers for a second.

There was something in his stare—something resolute, unwavering and it sent a shiver through her. She had to look away, had to break the spell cast over her the moment he'd walked into the room.

Was she kidding? He'd cast a spell on her the moment he'd landed in India and railroaded her trip.

Lowering his glass, he placed it on a nearby table and did the same with hers before leaning forward, way too close.

'Tell me. Is my being here making you uncomfortable?'

'A little.'

She settled for the truth, hating how gauche and floundering and out of her depth he made her feel. She hadn't asked for this, hadn't fostered this attraction or encouraged it but it was there all the same, buzzing between them, electrifying and alive, no matter how hard she tried to ignore it.

'Why?'

He didn't back away. If anything, he leaned closer and her skin tingled where his shirt cuff brushed her wrist.

'Because you're the type of guy any woman in her right mind should stay away from,' she blurted, silently cringing at her brusque outburst.

Rather than offending him, he laughed, the rich, deep chuckles as warm and seductive as the rest of him.

'You keep coming back to that playboy thing. Don't believe everything you hear.'

She raised an eyebrow. 'So you're not a ladies' man?'

'Let's just say my reputation may be embroidered somewhat.'

His laconic response drew a smile. While Ethan was trying to downplay his reputation, she had little doubt every word was true. She'd seen his passing parade of women, either in the tabloids or at the restaurant, and while she should be the last person to judge who he paired up with—look at the monumental mistake she'd made in marrying Richard—the vacuous women didn't seem his type.

'It really bothers you, doesn't it? My past?'

She shrugged. 'None of my business.'

'I'd like it to be.'

He was so close now, his breath feathered over her cheek and she held her breath, wanting to move away, powerless to do so with her muscles locked in shock.

If she turned her head a fraction, he'd kiss her. His intent was clear—his words, his closeness, his body language—and she exhaled softly, her body quivering with the need to be touched, her heart yelling *no, no, not him!*

Rivers of heat flowed from her fingertips to her toes, searing a path through parts of her she'd forgotten existed. Her body blazed with it, lit up from within and in that instant her resolve was in danger of going up in flames.

'Tell me what you want, Tam.'

The fire fizzed and spluttered and died a slow, reluctant death as reality hit.

She knew what she wanted: to build a new life, to move forward, without the encumbrance of a man.

Yet she was wavering, seriously contemplating giving in to her irrational attraction for a man—not just any man, a man totally wrong for her.

That thought was enough to snap her out of the erotic spell he'd wound around them and she leaned back, forcing a laugh to cover the relief mingled with regret that she'd come to her senses in time.

'I want to take a look at that gorgeous brochure. So hand it over.'

He let her get away with it, but not before she saw the glitter of promise in his eyes.

This wasn't the end of it—far from it.

Ethan waved the brochure at Tam, snatching it away as she reached for it, laughing at her outrage.

He'd wanted her to say those three magical words—*I want you*—three little words that would've given him the go-ahead to seduce her in this exquisite room, a memory to last her a lifetime.

He wasn't a romantic, far from it, but he wanted her first time with him to be special, something she'd remember when they parted back in Melbourne.

After what she'd been through, she deserved special. Hell, she deserved the world on a plate and then some.

'Give me that!'

He raised the brochure higher. 'Uh-uh. Not until you ask nicely.'

She made a grab for it, leaning over far enough that the front of her robe parted and gave him a glimpse at heaven, her breasts lush and free and begging to be touched.

He swallowed, the game he was playing taking on new meaning as she leaned closer, reaching further, his lust skyrocketing as her tantalising exposed skin came within licking reach…

'Hand it over.' Laughing, she added, 'Pretty pleeeease,' before making a frantic lunge at his arm stretched overhead.

That last grab was her undoing, and his, as she teetered on her knees, precariously balanced, before tumbling against him and knocking him flat on his back on the sofa.

'Oops, sorry.'

Staring up at her, propped over him, her palms splayed against his chest, her mouth inches from his, her eyes wide and luminous and darkening with desire, she didn't look sorry in the least.

The brochure fluttered to the floor, forgotten, as she poised over him, hovered for an endless tension-fraught moment before lowering her head and slamming her mouth on his, eager, hungry, desperate.

He didn't know what shocked him more: the sheer reckless abandon with which she kissed him or the yearning behind it as her lips skidded over his, craving purchase, demanding he respond.

He didn't need to be asked twice, opening his mouth, the thrill of her tongue plunging in and exploring him tearing a groan from deep within.

How many times had he fantasised about having her?

But never in his wildest dreams had he envisioned her like this: crazy with passion, commanding, on top and totally in control.

Realisation slammed into him as she eased the kiss, lifted her head to stare at him with adoration in her glistening green eyes.

He wasn't in control any more, had lost it the second she'd pinned him down and initiated the kiss, demanding a response he was all too willing to give, but at what cost?

If losing control wasn't bad enough, the clear message in her eyes was.

She cared.

Too much.

He should've known a woman like her wouldn't respond physically to him unless she made an emotional connection and, by his own foolishness in encouraging deeper conversations, she had, damn it.

He wanted her so badly his body throbbed with it but this was all wrong.

It had to be on his terms, with her fully aware of what she was getting into, without hope in her heart and stars in her eyes.

Placing his hands around her waist, he lifted her so he could sit up, releasing her when they sat side by side.

Confusion clouded her eyes, with just a hint of hurt, but he couldn't acknowledge that, otherwise he'd find himself right back where he'd started, offering comfort when he shouldn't, giving her the wrong idea.

'What's wrong?'

'Nothing.'

He stood and strode to the door, needing to retreat before she pushed for answers he wasn't willing to give.

'I thought that's what you wanted.'

Her voice trembled, giving him another kick in the guts and he clenched his hands, thrust them into his pockets to stop himself from heading back to the sofa, sweeping her into his arms, carrying her to that tempting king-size bed and showing her exactly what he wanted.

'What about what you want?'

'That's pretty obvious. At least, I thought it was. Maybe I've been out of practice too long.'

He jammed his fists further in his pockets, rocked by the relentless urge to go to her.

She sounded so sad, so confused, and it was his fault.

He needed to get out of here. Now.

Spinning to face her, he strode back to the sofa, picked up the brochure lying at her feet and placed it on her lap when she didn't make a move to take it.

'Here's what you want.' He stabbed a finger at the glossy image of the Taj Mahal. 'I'm just a pushy guy bustling in on your dream.'

Her accusatory glare cut deep and he hated himself for putting her—them—in this position.

'I don't understand.'

Unable to resist dropping one last swift kiss on her lips, he muttered, 'Neither do I,' as he headed for the door.

CHAPTER SIX

TAMARA still didn't understand the next day when they reached Bharatpur.

She'd spent a sleepless night, analysing the moment Ethan had pulled away, over and over, replaying it until she'd turned over and stuffed her face into the pillow to block out the memory.

She'd kissed him, he'd pulled away.

No matter how many times she went over it in her head, it all came back to that.

It didn't make any sense. The way he'd been flirting, the way he'd been charming her from the moment she'd walked into Ambrosia and found him there, the way he'd been kissing her, repeatedly...

Something wasn't right and, in the wee small hours of the morning, she'd come to a decision.

Forget the humiliation, forget the embarrassing kiss, forget she'd made a fool of herself.

This trip was too important to let one cringe-worthy moment tarnish it. She'd waited too long to take it, was finally discovering her old self beneath layers of battered esteem.

And she liked what she was discovering: that she could feel again, that being with a man could be pleasurable rather than horrifying, that she liked feeling like a desirable woman rather than an ornamental wife brought out of her box to perform on cue at dinner parties and shelved the rest of the time.

If that scared Ethan, tough.

Maybe the guy was too used to getting his own way, was one of those strong guys who preferred to do all the chasing? Well, he could keep chasing, for that was the first and last time she showed him how amazing she found this irrational, incongruous attraction.

She should be glad he'd back-pedalled today, had made urbane small talk and eased off the flirting on their trip here, had made it perfectly clear he didn't want to discuss his about-face last night.

Instead, she found herself darting curious glances at him, trying to read his rigid expression—and failing—somewhat saddened by their long lapses into silence.

'Your chariot…'

Ethan gestured at the rickshaw he'd hired to take them around Keoladeo Ghana National Park, Bharatpur's famous bird sanctuary, and she smiled, relieved, when he responded with one of his own.

Buoyed by the first sign of anything other than irresolute self-control, she said, 'Chariot, huh? Does that make you Prince Charming?'

He shook his head, but not before she glimpsed his familiar rakish smile, her heart flip-flopping against her will in response.

'What is it with girls and princes?'

She could've elaborated on the whole 'being swept off their feet, rescued and living happily ever after' scenario girls loved from the moment they could walk. But considering her fantasy had evaporated quicker than Richard's love for her, she shrugged and stepped up into the tiny rickshaw. Her relief at being sheltered from the relentless sun instantly evaporated as he swung up beside her and she realised how small these rickshaws really were.

'Let's get moving. I don't want to spend too long here when we've got the Taj this afternoon.'

She agreed, though his brisk tone implied he couldn't wait to get to the end of this trip, couldn't get away from her quick enough.

She wasn't going to overanalyse this, remember? Wasn't going to waste time trying to read his mind or figure out his motivations.

'Can't wait.'

After instructing the driver to go, he leaned back, his thigh brushing hers, his arm wedged against hers as she wished her fickle body would stay with the programme.

This was a transient attraction, a natural reaction of her hormones considering she hadn't been with a man for almost two years. Richard hadn't touched her during that last year of their marriage, and she hadn't wanted him to. It made her skin crawl just thinking about where he'd been at the time, who he'd been with.

Silence stretched taut between them and she needed to say something—anything—to distract from her skin prickling with awareness where it touched his.

'My mum talked about the Taj constantly. About its inception, its history, but she never got to see it. This was going to be her first time…'

Her breath hitched on a part sob and she clamped her lips shut, wishing he'd sling an arm across her shoulders and cradle her close. He'd been nothing but comforting the last time she'd spoken about Khushi, had encouraged her to do so.

But, despite the momentary flicker of compassion in his eyes, the flash of understanding, he remained impassive, jaw clenched so hard the muscles bulged.

'You'll get to see it through her eyes, through her stories. You may be the one standing before it today but she'll be the one bringing it alive for you.'

She raised her gaze to his, emotion clogging her throat, tears stinging her eyes, but he glanced away, leaving her torn between wanting to hug him for saying something so perfect and throttle him for cheapening it by looking away.

'Thanks, I needed to hear that.'

'My pleasure.'

Empty words, considering there was nothing remotely pleasurable about the barrier he'd erected between them, the severing of an emotional connection no matter how tentative.

She'd been frozen inside for years, emotionally frigid as she'd shut down to cope with Richard's psychological abuse, numbing her feelings to stop the constant barrage of verbal put-downs and criticism.

She'd thought she was incapable of feeling anything again, yet Ethan had given her that gift.

Despite the urge to go running and screaming in the opposite direction, the more he charmed her, despite the fear that her body was responding to him and overthrowing her mind, despite the paralysing terror of feeling anything for a man ever again, she'd allowed him to get close enough to melt the icy kernel surrounding her heart and, for that, she was eternally grateful.

Her lower lip wobbled at the thought of how far she'd come and she blinked, inhaled sharply, her senses slammed by his sandalwood scent from the hotel's luxurious selection of complimentary toiletries, as she savoured the illicit pleasure of being this close to him.

With a small shake of her head, she pulled a guidebook from her bag and rattled open the pages, desperate for a diversion from her thoughts, her emotions and the uneasy silence.

'It says here this place is a bird paradise, with over three hundred and eighty species, including some rare Siberian cranes.'

He turned, leaned over her shoulder, peered at the book and

she held her breath, unprepared for all that hard male chest to be wedged up against her.

'What else have they got?'

Forced to breathe in order to answer him, she inhaled another heady lungful of pure male tinged with sandalwood, momentarily light-headed. Her palms were clammy, her body on fire and her head spun with the implications of how she was reacting to him, despite all her self-talk that she shouldn't.

Peering at the guidebook as if it had all the answers to questions she shouldn't even be contemplating, she cleared her throat.

'Hawks, pelicans, geese, eagles among countless other species, and they also have golden jackals, jungle cats, striped hyenas, blackbuck and wild boar.'

'Great.'

Yeah, great. He'd hired the rickshaw driver for an hour and in that time she'd be stuck here, nice and tight, unable to breathe without his tantalising scent assailing her, unable to move without encountering way too much firm muscle, unable to think without rehashing reasons why this could be better if he opened up and she shed her inhibitions.

As a pelican flew at the rickshaw in an indignant rage, the driver swerved, throwing her flush against Ethan and all that glorious hard muscle.

Righting her, he smiled, a warm, toe-curling smile that reached down to her heart, the type of smile that made resistance futile, the first genuine smile he'd given her all day.

Desperate to prolong the moment now she'd finally seen a glimpse of the old Ethan, she said, 'No need to throw myself at you, huh?'

Her hands splayed against his chest, the rhythmic pounding of his heart proof that he was as affected by their proximity as her.

'You don't hear me complaining.'

He held her gaze and she couldn't speak, couldn't breathe,

the distant screech of an eagle as hauntingly piercing and achingly poignant as the sudden yearning to stay like this, touching him, secure in his arms, for more than a brief moment.

She wanted to push him for answers, to ask why he'd gone cold on her but, as much as her foolhardy heart urged her, she couldn't do it.

She'd taken a risk on a man once before and her judgement had been way off. She'd thought Richard had been a safe bet, she'd trusted him and look how that had turned out. Trusting Ethan would be tantamount to handing him her heart on a serving platter complete with carving knives.

As she tried to muster a response, he straightened her, putting her away from him with strong yet gentle hands. 'You know what you look like?'

'What?'

'A worm surrounded by the entire population of this bird sanctuary.'

He tucked a strand of hair behind her ear, allowed his fingers to linger, brushing the soft skin of her neck. 'I'm not going to bite, Tam. So quit looking at me like I'm the big bad wolf.'

Before she could respond, he ducked his head, captured her mouth in a swift, urgent kiss that barely lasted a second, leaving her dazed and stunned and more baffled than ever.

'Though I have to say, you'd look great in red.'

With that, he turned to watch a gaggle of geese take flight as she sat there, bracing her feet to stop herself from rocking against him any more than necessary, absolutely speechless, thoroughly perplexed, and touching her trembling lips with a shaky hand.

He confounded, mystified and thoroughly bamboozled her, blowing hot and cold just like his employees said and, right now, she wanted to be like those geese. Free to take off, free to expand her wings, free to be whoever she wanted to be.

She wanted to feel carefree and light-hearted and unburdened for the first time in years, wanted to have the courage to explore outside her comfort zone, to let the winds of chance take her wherever.

Darting a quick glance at Ethan, still staring resolutely out the other side, she knew with the utmost certainty that he was a part of that yearning to explore the unknown, the craving to take a chance, no matter how much his behaviour bewildered her.

She was so used to repressing her true feelings, so used to playing a part, that she didn't know who she was any more, let alone how to be the carefree, happy woman she'd once been.

Ethan could help her.

He could help her rediscover her zing, could nurture their spark towards something exciting, something beyond her wildest dreams.

But she had to take a chance.

Was she willing to take a risk for a fleeting happiness that would dissolve when Ethan stepped on a plane bound for Melbourne?

Some choice and, as the rickshaw bumped and rocked and swayed through the sanctuary, she knew she'd have to make up her mind and fast. They had half a day and one night left together. Not a heck of a lot of time to make a decision.

Chance. Risk. Gamble. Venture.

Things she'd never done when married to Richard, content in the security he'd provided, when she'd been the dutiful wife so in love with her husband she'd been blinded to his faults until it was too late.

But that part of her life was over, her dreams of happily ever after shattered by a selfish egomaniac, and for the first time in years she could do as she damn well pleased.

Stakes were high.

Make a mistake and she'd lose the tentative friendship she'd developed with Ethan, something she'd grown to depend on over the last week.

Make it work and they could shoot to the moon and back.

With a heartfelt sigh she sat back, braced against the rocking, and watched the geese fly higher and higher, reaching for the stars.

Maybe she should too.

CHAPTER SEVEN

'YOU ready?'

Tamara nodded, took a deep breath and opened her eyes, the air whooshing out of her lungs as she caught her first unforgettable glimpse of the Taj Mahal.

The incredible monument shimmered in the early dusk, its white marble reflecting in the long moat in front of it, casting a ghostly glow over the magical gardens surrounding it.

'It's something else.'

She glanced at Ethan, too choked to speak, grateful he knew how much this moment meant to her.

Sliding an arm around her waist, he hugged her close. 'Your mum's here with you. She'd want you to enjoy this, to be happy.'

Gnawing on her bottom lip to keep from blubbering, she searched his eyes, wondering if he knew how much of an integral part he played in her happiness these days.

All she saw in those fathomless blue depths was caring, compassion and a tenderness that took her breath away.

Thankfully, they'd broken the ice following the rickshaw ride and, while he hadn't slipped back into full-on flirting just yet, she had hopes that their last kiss hadn't ruined their friendship for ever.

For no matter how many logical, sane reasons she'd pondered as to why they couldn't be anything more than friends, they all faded into oblivion the second she caught her first breathtaking glimpse of the Taj.

There was nowhere else she'd rather be this very moment than right here, with this man.

Placing a hand on his cheek, she caressed the stubble, enjoying the light prickle rasping against her palm.

'I hope you know that sharing this with you is beyond special.'

Surprise flickered in his eyes—surprise tinged with wariness.

'I'm a poor stand-in for your mum but I'm glad I can be here for you.'

He semi-turned, forcing her to drop her hand, and she followed his line of vision, blown away by the fact that she was standing in front of one of the new Seven Wonders of the World, the River Yamuna flowing tranquilly nearby, surrounded by fellow tourists yet feeling as if she were the only woman in the world to have ever felt this incredible in the face of such beauty.

'It's stood the test of time, hasn't it?'

She followed his line of vision, taking in the curved dome, the archways, the exquisite ornamentation. 'Considering it took twenty-two years to build, I guess they made it to last.'

He did a slow three-sixty, taking in the gardens, the fountains, before fixing his gaze on the Taj again. 'I knew it'd be impressive but I didn't expect anything like this.'

'I know,' she breathed on a sigh, closing her eyes for a second, savouring the moment, elated that when she opened them again she'd see the same incredible sight. 'Do you know the story behind it?'

He held up his hand; it wavered from side to side. 'A little. Shah Jahan, a Mughal Emperor, had it constructed in memory of his beloved wife Mumtaz Mahal. Took about twenty thousand workers, a thousand elephants to haul materials and used about twenty-eight precious and semi-precious stones to do the inlay work.'

She smiled. 'Someone's been reading their Lonely Planet guide.'

He raised an eyebrow. 'Okay, Miss Smarty Pants. Why don't you tell me what you know?'

'My version reads like a romance novel.'

'I'm a sensitive New Age guy. Go ahead. Try me.'

'Okay, but you'd better sit down. This could take a while.' She sank onto the ground, clasped her hands around her knees and rested her chin on her knees, waiting until he sat to begin.

'Shah Jahan was the son of the fourth Mughal emperor of India. He was fourteen when he met Arjumand Banu Begum, a Muslim Persian princess, who was fifteen. It was love at first sight.'

She sighed, wondering what it would be like to be swept away like that, to know in an instant you were destined to be with that person.

Richard had charmed and blustered and cajoled his way into her affections, offering her the safety of marriage, a safety she'd craved since her dad had died. Yes, it had been quick and, yes, she'd fallen hard but nothing like locking eyes with a person and knowing with the utmost certainty he was *the one*.

'But they were kids! That's not even legal.'

She waved away his protest. 'Different times. We're talking about the early sixteen hundreds. Do you want to hear the rest or not?'

'Go ahead. I can see you're busting to tell me.'

Sending him a mock frown, she continued. 'After meeting the princess, Shah Jahan went back to his father and declared he wanted to marry her. They married five years later. When he became emperor eleven years later, he entrusted her with the royal seal and gave her the title Mumtaz Mahal, which means "jewel of the palace". Though he had other wives—'

'That's not romance, that's bigamy.'

She rolled her eyes. 'That's allowed in his religion. Anywaaaay—'

He grinned at her obvious annoyance at his constant interruptions.

'She was his favourite, accompanied him everywhere, even on military campaigns. But when she was giving birth to their fourteenth child—' Ethan winced and she couldn't blame him '—there were complications and she died. Apparently, legend has it that she secured a promise from him with her last breath to build a beautiful monument in her memory.'

She gestured to the Taj Mahal. 'And he did.'

Her glance roved over the towering dome, the intricate archways, the cypress trees nearby, as she pondered the depth of that kind of love, captivated by the spellbinding romance of it all.

'That's some story.'

He stared at the monument, the sudden tension in his shoulders alerting her to the fact that something bothered him, before swiftly turning to her and fixing her with a probing stare.

'Do you believe in love at first sight?'

At that moment, with his intense blue eyes boring into hers, his forearm brushing hers, his heat radiant and palpable and real, she wished she did.

'My parents did. They took one look at each other on Colva beach and fell in love.'

He didn't let her off that easily. 'I didn't ask about them. I'm asking you.'

Here was her chance to tell him she'd been thinking about pushing the boundaries, possibly seeing where it could take them.

But the reservations of a lifetime dogged her. She'd always done the right thing, been the dutiful daughter, the good little wife. She didn't like rocking the boat, changing the status quo. She'd tried it once before, was still dealing with the consequences.

Drawing a harsh, shaky breath, she forced her fingers to relax rather than leave welts from digging into her hands.

'I don't know what I believe any more.'

He shook his head, disappointment clouding his eyes. 'That's a cop-out.'

'Pardon?'

'You heard me. You're a strong, resilient woman. You've coped with losing your husband. You've made decisions to move forward with your life. Plans to return to work.' He jerked his head towards the Taj Mahal. 'Coming here.'

He laid a hand on her arm and she started. 'All major decisions—but see that? The way you just jumped when I touched you?' He shook his head, his mouth twisting with disappointment as he released her. 'You're selling yourself short there. You're not being honest.'

She leaped to her feet, needing space, a continent's worth to flee the truth of his words and the reckless pounding of her heart.

'This isn't about honesty. It's about taking a risk and I hate taking risks.'

When a passing couple stared, she ran a weary hand over her face, lowered her voice.

'I'm not like you. You're brave. Fearless. Take charge. Everything so clear in black and white. While I feel like I've been living in some alternate grey universe and I'm finally coming out the other side.'

He stood, reached for her but she held him away. 'No, let me finish. I need to say this. You're successful, accomplished, but you know what I envy the most? You know who you are. You know your place in the world and, right now, that's something I don't have a clue about…'

Her declaration petered out on a whisper, a taut silence

stretching between them until she wished he'd say something—anything—to fill the tense void.

Finally, he slid an arm around her waist, pulled her close, and she let him.

'I didn't know.'

'That I'm such a sad case?'

Her attempt at humour fell flat.

'That you felt like that. I'm sorry.'

'Don't be. It's something I have to work through.'

Something she was determined to do. Everything seemed much easier here, away from the memories of Richard, of discovering the truth.

'You've had a rough trot. You know you deserve to be happy, right?'

She'd spent years pretending she was happy when she was anything but: pretending Richard's passive-aggressive barbs didn't hurt, pretending his criticism was well-intended, pretending she still loved him when inside she'd died a little every day.

The pretence had extended following his death, playing the grieving widow for appearance's sake when deep down she'd felt like screaming at his treachery, at his selfishness in making her life miserable while he had a ball with another woman behind her back.

'I want to be happy…'

'Then let go.'

She knew what he was implying, could read it in every tense line of his body.

Meeting his unwavering stare, she suppressed her inner voice screaming, *no, no, don't do it.*

'With you?'

He nodded slowly, his eyes never leaving hers. 'Want to know why I came on this trip?'

'I thought it was all business?'

He smiled at her soft sarcasm, his expression inscrutable. 'Because of you.'

He gripped her arms, his fierceness so overwhelming she would've taken a step back if he wasn't hanging on to her.

'Then why do you keep pulling away? It's like you get too close and then—wham, nothing.'

He shook his head, his hands tightening their grip as he hauled her closer. 'I barely knew you before this trip and spending time with you changed everything. Yeah, I'm a red-blooded male and I want you. But now—'

He searched her eyes for—what? Approval? Some sign that she wanted to see this through until the end?

'What do you want from me now?'

'This.'

Before she could make sense of his words, before she could push him for an explanation, his mouth swooped and captured hers in a hungry, rash kiss, blindingly brilliant in its savage intensity.

Her senses reeled as he deepened the kiss, as she let him, stunned by the ferocity of her own response as she grabbed frantically at his T-shirt, clung to him, dragged him closer.

If he'd slowed down, been tender and gentle rather than commanding and masterful, she would've had time to think, time to dredge up every rational reason why she shouldn't be doing this after the way he'd rebuffed her last night.

Instead, she let go, became herself, not some mouse-like woman worried about what other people would think of her for staying in a loveless marriage with a heartless tyrant if they knew.

Her knees wobbled as he pulled her closer, his hands strumming her back, his lips playing delightful havoc with hers as he challenged her with every tantalising sweep of his tongue, with every searing brush of his lips.

It was the kiss of a lifetime.

A kiss filled with promise and excitement and wonder, without a shade of grey in sight.

A kiss memories were made of.

An eternity later, when the initial blistering heat subsided and their lips eased, lingered, before releasing, the reality of the situation rushed in, the old self-doubts swamping her in a crushing wave.

'Don't do that.'

He tipped her chin up, caressed her bottom lip with his thumb. 'Don't go second-guessing yourself or what just happened.'

'I'm not—'

His mouth kicked up into the roguish smile she loved so much. 'This is me you're talking to.'

'That's what I'm afraid of,' she murmured, smoothing his T-shirt where she'd gripped it so hard she'd wrinkled it to the point where it needed a shot of steam or two to de-crease.

'Just take that kiss at face value, as a first step.'

She was almost too afraid to ask. 'A first step to what?'

Brushing a soft, barely-there kiss across her lips, he said, 'That's something we're about to find out.'

CHAPTER EIGHT

As FAR as first dates went, Ethan couldn't fault this one. He leaned back on outstretched arms and looked up at the monstrous India Gate in the centre of New Delhi.

In reality, he could've been in a dingy alleyway in the back of Timbuktu and the date would've been amazing all the same, courtesy of the stunning woman by his side, looking happy and more relaxed than he'd ever seen her.

'What are you thinking?'

Tamara smiled up at him from her vantage point, stretched out on the grass on propped elbows.

'I'm thinking if I see one more monument or fort or palace I'll go cross-eyed.'

He laughed, reached out to pluck a blade of grass stuck to her hair. 'But this is the Arc de Triomphe of India. It commemorates the seventy thousand Indian soldiers who died fighting for the British Army in World War One and is inscribed with the names of over thirteen thousand British and Indian soldiers killed in the 1919 Afghan war.'

She shook her head. 'There you go again, swallowing another guidebook. You know, all those facts will give you indigestion.'

He winked, ducked his head for a quick kiss that left her blushing. 'Just trying to impress you.'

'You've done that already.'

Her praise, the easy way she admitted it, warmed his heart, before stabbing doubt daggers into it again.

He'd tried his best to back off, to subdue his panic, to alienate her.

It had worked for a while; he'd regained control but it hadn't eradicated the fear.

The fear that he was already feeling way too much, the fear that what was happening between them was beyond anything he'd ever felt before but, most of all, the fear that no matter what he did, how hard he tried to stay in command, his over-whelming need for this woman would engulf him anyway.

He wanted this—right? Then why the constant nagging deep in his gut that this was more than he could handle?

During his relentless pursuit, he hadn't actually spelled it out that he wasn't interested in a relationship. He hoped to date for a while, have some fun together, explore the under-lying spark simmering between them.

But that was where things ended. Would Tam want more? He doubted it, considering she'd talked about new begin-nings, a fresh start. Believing her only encouraged him to indulge their attraction, guilt-free.

If things got too heavy, he knew what he had to do: run, just like his mum.

He'd loved her, had been secure she returned the sentiment until his childish delusions had been ripped from under him, leaving him a homeless orphan with a mother who'd rather be on her own than stuck with a five-year-old.

'What's wrong?'

He blinked, wrenched back to the present by her tentative question, her hand on his arm, and he mentally dusted himself off.

Today wasn't a day for sour memories.

Today was a day for creating brilliant new ones.

'Just thinking about where we go from here.'

It wasn't a lie exactly. He'd been stewing over their future since they'd opened an emotional Pandora's Box at the Taj yesterday.

He wanted this, wanted more than friendship with this incredibly special woman. Then why couldn't he rid himself of the faintest mantra stuck on rewind in the back of his mind, the one that chanted *be careful what you wish for?*

He'd always been ambitious, driven to succeed, craving control to stave off the darkness that crept into his soul at the oddest of times—a darkness filled with depressing memories of physical abuse and living on the streets and starving to the point of desperation.

Being one hundred per cent focused on business had served him just fine. Until now, when his legendary control was smashed like a soup tureen by a temperamental chef by taking the next step with Tam.

He half expected her to balk at the question, to shirk it. Instead, she fixed him with those mesmerising green eyes, eyes he could happily get lost in for ever.

'Honestly? I have no idea. I'm in Goa for the next week. You're here on business.'

She idly plucked at the grass beneath her hands, picking blades and letting them fall. 'I guess we wait until we're back in Melbourne and see what happens.'

For some strange reason her answer filled him with relief when he should be pushing her, ensuring she wouldn't back off once their journey together ended today.

What the hell was happening to him?

Sure, he enjoyed the thrill of the chase as much as the next guy but usually didn't tire of something once possessed—until the woman in question wanted to possess him. So why was he feeling like this? So uncertain, so uneasy, so unhinged.

His goal had been to seduce her and he was almost there. Then why the unrelenting fear he'd got more than he'd bargained for?

'You're not happy about that?'

He forced a smile, tension sneaking up the back of his neck and bringing on one of the classic headaches reserved for day-long meetings.

'We've come a long way in a week. Maybe things will be different when we get home.'

A tiny frown puckered her brow as she pushed up to a sitting position. 'That's not like you. You're the optimistic one. I'm the confirmed pessimist.'

What could he say?

That he didn't want a full-blown relationship? That he didn't trust what they had? That he didn't trust easily, period?

Reaching out, she draped a hand over his, squeezed softly. 'There's more. Tell me.'

If he looked for excuses long enough he'd find them and at that moment a veritable smorgasbord flooded his mind, leaving him to choose the juiciest one.

'The press hounded you for weeks after Richard's death. What do you think they'll do when they discover we're dating?'

Her frown intensified as her hand slid off his. 'They'll probably say I'm some kind of trumped up tart who waited until her dearly beloved husband was cold in the ground for a year before moving on from the chef to the billionaire res-taurateur where he worked. So what? It's all nonsense. Who cares what they say?'

But she was worried. He saw it in the telltale flicker in her eyes, in the pinched mouth.

If Tam had put up with the constant publicity barrage being married to Rich entailed, she had to care about appearances and, no matter how much she protested now, he knew the first hint of scandal in the tabloids back home would send her scut-tling for cover.

Where would that leave him? Content to sit back and watch from the sidelines? He'd be damned if he settled for that again.

'As long as you're sure—'

'Of course I'm not sure!'

She jumped to her feet, eyes flashing, hands clenched, more irritated than he'd ever seen her.

'But you wanted this—*you*. You pushed me. You chased and pulled back several times, confusing the heck out of me until I couldn't think straight but I'm still here.'

She stabbed a finger in his direction, glared at him, all bristling indignation and fiery righteousness, and he'd never seen anything so beautiful.

'Now I'm ready to take a chance on us, you start hedging. What's with that?' She ended on a half sob and he leaped to his feet and reached for her.

'Don't, just don't.'

She held up her hands to ward him off and he couldn't blame her.

He was still a screwup. No matter how far he'd come from that lonely, desperate, filthy street kid who'd scrounged food scraps to survive, no matter how rich or successful, he was still the same wary guy who wouldn't let anyone get too close, let alone a woman.

But he had to fix this, and fast, before he not only ruined any chance they had of dating but shot down their new friendship too.

'Tam, listen to me. I—'

'Why should I? Give me one good reason why I should listen to you?'

She folded her arms, glared, her stoic expression at odds with her trembling mouth, and it took every ounce of self-control not to bundle her into his arms.

He held his hands out to her, palms up, and shrugged. 'Because I care about you.'

She wrinkled her nose. 'Care, right. Well, you know what? If you cared, you wouldn't say you want one thing, act another when you get it. I'm sick of it.'

Tears glistened in her eyes, turning them a luminous green and slugging him harder than his first shot of alcohol as a shivering fourteen-year-old squatting in a Melbourne hovel, desperate to stay warm.

Shaking her head, she swiped a hand over her eyes, sniffed. 'I don't need this. I didn't ask for it, I didn't want it, but at least I had the guts to take a chance, so I'll be damned if I stand here and let you play me for a fool.'

'I'm not—'

'You are.'

If she'd shouted, ranted, abused him, he might've stood a chance at convincing her otherwise but her soft, empty words, frigid with contempt, reached icy fingers down to his soul, freezing what little hope he had left.

'You've got a week to figure out what you want.'

He reached for her hand, briefly capturing her fingertips before she snatched it away.

'Tam, don't do this.'

She straightened, fixed him with a superior glare at odds with her shaky hands. 'Do what? Stand up for myself? Speak my mind?'

Her mouth twisted into a wry grimace. 'This is *my* time now. Time I start looking after number one, and that's me.'

She shook her head, gathered her hair, piled it into a loose bun on top of her head before letting it tumble around her shoulders again. He loved watching her do it, an absent-minded habit she did when thinking or uptight.

'I just want to make sure you know what you're getting yourself into. As far as I know, I'm the first guy you've dated since Rich and that's got to be a big step for you.'

'But it's my step to take!'

He'd never seen her so irate and for a moment he wondered if there was more behind her flare-up. Was she nervous and covering it with bluster? Or was she as crazy for him as he was for her and had no idea how to control it, just like him?

'You know, for the first time in forever, I felt safe yesterday. At first I thought it was the Taj, the overwhelming sense of calm that flowed through me when I stepped inside. But it wasn't just that.'

She raised her wide-eyed gaze to his, her unguarded expression beseeching him to understand. And he did, all too well. Tam needed a man to make her feel secure, to cherish her, to spoil her, to do all the things Rich had done.

But he couldn't be that man.

He couldn't relinquish control of anything, let alone lose it over a woman, no matter how special. However, now wasn't the time to get into all that. The way things were heading, it looked like their first date may also be their last.

'It was you, Ethan. You being there with me, sharing it, treating me like a woman…'

She trailed off, shrugged and took a step backwards. 'Maybe it was just the monument, after all.'

'Tam, look—'

She raised her hand—to ward him off? To say goodbye?

'I'll see you in Melbourne.'

While his heart urged him to follow her, to tell her the truth, to make her understand, his feet were rooted to the spot as he watched the woman who'd captured his heart without trying walk away.

CHAPTER NINE

TAMARA slid her sunglasses into place, tucked the latest crime novel under her arm, slung her towel over her shoulder and headed for the beach.

She'd been in Goa two days—two long days when she'd spent every waking moment touring around, filling the hours with sights and sounds of her mum's birthplace.

'Prawns today, missie?'

Smiling, she stopped at one of the many food vendors scattered along the roadside leading to Colva Beach. She'd been starving when she'd arrived here her first day and the tantalising aroma of seafood sizzling in garlic and turmeric had led her straight here.

'Two, please.'

She held up two fingers for reinforcement, knowing the wizened old man would give her four, just like he had the previous times she'd stopped here. Not that she was complaining but the waistbands of her skirts sure were.

His wide toothless grin warmed her heart as she handed over the rupees and juggled the hot prawns, waving the skewer around and blowing on them before biting into the delicious crispy flesh, savouring the freshness of the seafood drenched in spicy masala.

She devoured the first prawn in two bites, saliva pooling

in her mouth at the anticipatory bite of the next as she strolled past another vendor selling a fiery fish vindaloo that smelled as good as the prawns.

'Tomorrow,' she mouthed to the hopeful guy whose face fell when she didn't stop.

Not that she wasn't tempted but at that moment her new friends caught sight of her and were busy hopping from one foot to the other in some bizarre welcoming dance that never failed to bring a smile to her face, and she had no option but to stop.

'You build?'

The eldest of the group of five kids, ranging from three to six, pointed to a makeshift bucket made from an old ghee tin while the rest dropped to their knees and started digging in the sand with their hands.

'Sure.'

She knelt, picked up the tin and started scooping, enjoying the hot sand beating down as she fell into a rhythm: scoop, pat, dump, scoop, pat, dump, listening to their excited chatter, unable to understand a word of the rapid Hindi but returning their blinding smiles as their castle grew.

Today, like the first day they'd beckoned her to join in their fun, she took simple pleasure in doing something associated with her childhood, the repetitive activity as soothing now as it had been then.

She'd built monstrous sandcastles after her dad had died, had poured all her energy into the task in an attempt to block out the pain. But, as the castles had grown, so had her resentment until she'd kicked them down, one crumbling turret at a time.

Yet she'd started building the moment her mum had taken her to the beach the next time, painstakingly erecting the towering castles, complete with shell windows and seaweed flags.

Until it hadn't hurt so much any more and she'd stopped kicking them down, happy to watch the sea gently wash away her creation.

It had taken time to release her resentment—at losing her dad, the unfairness of it—and now, with the sand trickling through her fingers, calmness stole over her, soothing the discontent gnawing at the edges of her consciousness since she'd arrived.

She'd tried ignoring it, had even tried meditating as darkness descended each evening and she sat in a comfy cane chair on her veranda looking out over peaceful Colva beach, her beach hut the perfect spot away from the madding crowds.

While the deliberate relaxation had gone a long way to soothing her weary soul, to banishing some of the anger and acrimony that had dogged her incessantly for the last year, it had also served to tear a new wound in her already bruised heart.

Thanks to Ethan.

Even now, she had no idea what had happened in the interim between their first kiss and her walking away from him in Delhi.

She'd often felt like that with Richard—lonely, as if floating on a sea of anonymity despite being constantly surrounded by his business acquaintances and friends. She'd been a part of his life, a fixture, like part of the furniture, smiling and chatting and playing the perfect hostess while inside she'd been screaming.

She hadn't told her mum about it. Khushi had lived through enough trauma of her own, had lost a husband, a country. Her mum had fussed over her enough when she was growing up, overprotective to the point of stifling at times. She'd understood it, her mum's need to hang on to the only family she had, and in her own way she'd wanted to return the favour.

She'd never spoken an ill word against Richard, despite her growing despair that her husband had morphed from a strong, steady man to a controlling, spoiled tyrant with a penchant for wine and women.

Losing her mum had been devastating but, considering what she'd learned about Richard when he'd died, a small part of her had been glad her mum hadn't been around to see it.

Bitterness had plagued her for the last year, yet over the last week it had ceased seeping into her soul and sapping her energy.

Because of Ethan.

Ethan, who by encouraging her to open her heart to him, only to hand it straight back to her, had now left her unhappier than ever.

He'd been relentless in his pursuit of her ever since they'd started this trip—discounting the occasional withdrawal—yet when she'd finally given in he'd retreated faster than a lobster sighting a bubbling bisque.

And she'd overreacted. Boy, had she overreacted and the memory of how she'd berated him made her knock over a turret or two as her hands turned clumsy.

The kids frowned as one and she shrugged in apology, intent on smoothing her side of the castle, wishing she could smooth over her gaffe with Ethan as easily.

She'd picked a fine time to rediscover her assertiveness and, while it had felt great standing up for herself and verbalising exactly how she was feeling, she'd chosen the wrong place, the wrong time, the wrong man.

He hadn't deserved her outpouring of anger any more than she'd deserved any of Richard's callous put-downs.

Shame she wouldn't get the chance to tell him, for she was under no illusions that, once they returned to Melbourne, Ethan would move onto his next challenge, relegating her to what? Distant acquaintance again? Friend?

Considering they hadn't been anything remotely near friends before this trip, she should be grateful. Instead, she couldn't help but wish she'd had a chance to rediscover another part of her identity: that of a desirable woman with needs desperate to be fulfilled.

Dusting off her hands, she stood, surveying their creation. The kids imitated her and she pointed at the lopsided castle and applauded them, charmed by their guileless giggles and high-fiving.

Everything was so simple for these kids: they had little, lived by the sea in makeshift shanties, shared a room with many siblings, had few toys, yet were happier than any kid she'd ever seen rollerblading or skateboarding in Melbourne.

Another lesson to be learned: keep things simple. She had once, content to curl up with a good romance novel, soft jazz in the background, a bowl of popcorn.

Living the high life, living a lie with Richard, had changed all that but it was time to get back to the basics. Her few days in Goa had taught her that if nothing else.

Waving goodbye to the kids, she set off for the shade of a nearby tree, throwing down her towel, smoothing it out and lying down, watching a couple stroll hand in hand down the beach.

She wanted to warn them that the first flush of love didn't last, that it soured and faded, no matter how committed the other person was to you.

She wanted to caution the beautiful young woman against giving too much of herself all in the name of love, wanted to alert her against loving too much to the point she risked losing herself.

She wanted to rant at the injustice of being a loyal, loving wife, only to have it all flung back in her face in the form of a six-foot Dutch ex-model with legs up to her neck and a dazzling smile.

But she didn't do any of that.

Instead, she slapped on her sun hat, flipped open her book and buried her nose in it. A much safer pastime than scaring young lovers and wasting time wishing she could change the past.

Ethan had enough business meetings to keep him busy for the next month.

This trip had been a success: he'd secured the chef he'd wanted and had put out feelers for a new flagship restaurant in Mumbai. He'd flown the length and breadth of India over the last two days, from Delhi to Mumbai to Chennai.

However, as he sat in the plush surrounds of the InterContinental Hotel in Chennai, he couldn't concentrate on business. Thoughts of Tam consumed him, as they had since she'd walked away from him in New Delhi.

He'd reached for his mobile phone numerous times, desperate to call her, to see how she was doing, to simply hear her voice. But he'd stopped each and every time, all too aware that ringing her would prove what he'd suspected for a while now—his legendary control was slipping.

Slipping? More like shot.

During their journey on the Palace of Wheels he'd dreamed of surprising her in Goa, of spending a leisurely week getting to know each other in every sense of the word.

So much for that dream.

'Ethan, my boy, good to see you.'

Dilip Kumar, his Indian representative in business matters, appeared out of nowhere, slapped him on the back as he stood. 'This is Sunil Bachnan, the investor we discussed on the phone last week.'

'Pleased to meet you.' He shook Sunil's hand, a giant of a man with a rounded belly protruding over his trousers, testament to a lifetime's worth of chappatis and dosais, the crispy rice pancakes filled with spicy potato he'd become addicted to.

'Likewise. I hear you're looking to open a restaurant here?'

He nodded, resumed his seat along with the other men, grateful to be back doing what he knew best. Business.

This he could manage. Unlike the rest of his life, which had spiralled dangerously out of control since he'd landed in this mystical country.

'Actually, I was thinking Mumbai. The growth there is staggering.'

Sunil gestured to a waiter for menus, nodded. 'The entire country is an economic boom. Pick a city, any city and your famous Ambrosia will do big business.' Patting his ample gut, he chortled. 'We love our food here in India.'

'You and me both.'

Though his appetite had vanished the last few days, a shame considering the array of amazing food on offer everywhere he went. For a guy who made his life out of food, he'd landed smack bang in food paradise.

'Right. Let's talk business as we eat.' Sunil rattled off an order in rapid Hindi to the hovering waiter as Dilip raised his beer. 'Cheers, my friend. And how is your travelling companion?'

'Good.'

He sculled half his beer in two gulps, wishing he hadn't opened his big mouth and mentioned Tam, not wanting to discuss her. The less he said the better, considering the constant repetition buzzing around his brain: replaying every scene of their trip, every hand touch, every smile, every kiss…

'You must bring her to dinner. My wife Sireesha will be thrilled to have you both—'

'Tamara's in Goa.'

Dilip's black eyes widened at his snapped response. 'I see.'

'Glad someone does,' he muttered into his beer glass, grateful that Sunil had answered a call on his mobile and wasn't privy to this conversation.

Trying to present a professional front to an investor sure as hell didn't involve discussing his non-existent love life.

'You and your lady friend are having problems?'

'Nothing I can't handle.'

Yeah, right, which was why he was on the east coast of India and Tam was on the west.

Dilip shook his head, steepled his fingers on his chest and

wobbled his head from side to side in a gesture he'd seen many times in India.

'If you permit me to be so bold, I have a story for you, my friend.'

Darting a frantic glance in Sunil's direction in the hope his phone call had ended, his heart sank as the investor held up a finger at him, pushed away from the table and headed for the foyer to continue his conversation.

'Look, Dilip, I'd rather focus on business—'

'Patience, my friend, patience.' He squeezed his eyes shut, as if trying to recall the story, before his bulging eyes snapped open and fixed on him. 'When I met my Sireesha, I was a penniless student and she was engaged to the son of a prominent doctor. Our paths crossed at university one day, when she dropped her books and I helped pick them up, and from that moment I knew she was the one for me.'

'And you're telling me this because?'

Dilip frowned, waggled a finger at him. 'Because I never wavered from my pursuit of her, no matter how unlikely it was we would ever be a couple. I was determined to have her and all the obstacles in our way were inconsequential.'

Ethan rubbed the back of his neck, shook his head. 'That's great but we're different. There are complications—'

'Complications, pah!'

Dilip waved his hand like a magician waving a wand. If only he could make all his problems disappear.

'The only complication is up here.' He tapped his head like an overzealous woodpecker. 'You think too much, you over-analyse, you lose.'

He pointed to his heart. 'You need to think with this. Let your heart rule your head. I know you are a brilliant business-man, so this will be foreign to you, yes?'

Hell, yeah. He never let his heart rule his head, not any more. His mum was the only woman who'd ever had a piece of his heart and she'd taken it with her the second she'd walked out of his life and left him to fend for himself, a bewildered five-year-old with no family, no money, no home.

'If you want her, this—' he tapped his heart '—needs to rule this.' He pointed to his head. 'Simple.'

Was it that simple?

Was he thinking too much, overanalysing everything, obstinately refusing to relinquish control despite the potentially incredible outcome?

What could be a greater incentive to lose control just a little than dating Tam?

Dilip snapped his fingers, jerked his head towards the door. 'Sunil is returning. For now, we do business. But later, my friend, you remember what I've said.'

He'd remember. But would he do anything about it?

Tamara needed a walk.

Her mum's cooking had been amazing but the authentic Goan cuisine she consumed way too much of at every meal was sublime.

She was particularly partial to bibinca, a rich sweet made from flour, sugar, ghee, coconut milk and about twenty egg yolks, baked and flavoured with nutmeg and cardamom.

Rich, delicious, addictive.

Exactly like Ethan, though his sweetness had evaporated around the time he'd stolen her hard-fought trust in him and flung it into the Ganges.

Picking up the pace, she headed for the water's edge, where the ocean tickled the sand, the only sound being the waves breaking gently on the shore.

Colva Beach was tranquil, lazy, the type of place to hang out the 'do not disturb' sign and just chill out. Her mum had said it was special but she'd always attributed her partiality to the fact she'd met her dad here. But mum had been right.

This place had an aura, a feeling, a sense that anything was possible, as she stared out over the endless ocean glowing turquoise in the descending dusk.

She slowed her pace, hitched up her peasant skirt and stepped into the waves, savouring the tepid water splashing about her ankles.

As a kid, she used to run through the shallows at St Kilda beach, jumping and splashing and frolicking, seeing how wet she could get, her folks strolling hand in hand alongside her, smiling indulgently.

They'd head to Acland Street afterwards, trawling the many cake shops, laughing as she'd pressed her face up to each and every window, trying to decide between melt-in-the-mouth chocolate éclairs or custard-oozing vanilla slices.

And later, much later, when her tummy was full and her feet dragging, she'd walk between them, each parent holding her hand, making her feel the luckiest little girl in the world.

A larger wave crashed into her legs, drenching the bottom half of her skirt and she laughed, the sound loud and startling in the silence.

How long since she'd laughed like that, truly laughed, totally spontaneous?

Ethan had made her laugh last week, several times... Shaking her head, she resisted the temptation to cover her ears with her hands.

Ethan, Ethan, Ethan—couldn't she focus on a new topic rather than the same old, same old?

With her skirt a dripping mess, she trudged up the beach, heading for her hut. Maybe a nice long soak in that killer tub filled with fragrant sandalwood oil would lull her into an Ethan-free zone?

As she scuffed her feet through the sand, a lone figure stepped onto the beach near her hut.

She wouldn't have paid much attention but for the breadth

of his shoulders, the familiar tilt of his head… She squinted, her pulse breaking into a gallop as the figure headed straight for her, increasingly recognisable with every determined stride.

It couldn't be.

It was.

In that instant, she forgot every sane reason why she should keep her distance from Ethan and ran towards him, sprinting, her feet flying across the sand as she hurtled herself into his open arms.

CHAPTER TEN

'Is THIS real?'

Ethan smoothed back her hair, caressed her cheek, his other hand holding her tight against him. 'Very.'

'What are you doing here?'

Tamara touched his face, her fingertips skimming his cheek, his jaw peppered in stubble, savouring the rasping prickle, still not believing this was real.

'I came to be with you.' He brushed his lips across hers—soft, tender, the barest of kisses that had her breath catching, along with her heart. 'There's nowhere else I'd rather be.'

She couldn't comprehend this. One minute she'd been alone and confused, the next he was here. For her.

'But after what happened in Delhi—'

'I was a fool.'

He clasped her face between his hands, his beseeching gaze imploring her to listen. 'I owe you an explanation.'

Her response of *you don't* died on her lips.

Considering the retreat and parry he'd been doing and the way they'd parted, he owed her that at least.

'Come on. I'm staying in that hut you just passed. We can talk there.'

She stepped out of his embrace but he swiftly pulled her

back into his arms, hugged her so fiercely the breath whooshed out of her lungs.

'Tam, I missed you.'

'Me too,' she murmured against his chest, her cheek happily squashed against all that lovely hard muscle.

Stroking her hair, he held her, their breathing in sync with their beating hearts, and for that one brief moment in time she understood the incredible power of the emotion that had drawn her mum and dad together on this very beach all those years ago.

There was something magical about this place, something transcendental and, as the first stars of the evening flickered overhead and the faintest tune of a soulful sitar drifted on the night air, she wondered if it was time to take a chance on love again.

'Any chance this hut of yours has a fully stocked fridge?' He patted his rumbling tummy. 'Feels like I haven't eaten in days.'

'Better than that. The hut is part of a resort so I put in an order for my meals first thing in the morning and they deliver.'

'Great. So what's for dinner?'

She laughed. 'You can take the boy out of the restaurant but you can't take the restaurant out of the boy.'

'Too right.' He slipped his hand in hers, squeezed. 'So, what's on for tonight?'

For an insane moment she could've sworn he wasn't talking about food as his steady blue-eyed gaze bored into hers, questioning, seeking, roguish. And, for the life of her, she couldn't remember what she'd ordered that morning.

Chuckling at her bemused expression, he fell into step beside her. 'Never mind, whatever it is I'll devour it.'

He paused, sent her a significant look. 'Happiness does that to a man. Gives him an appetite.'

'You're happy?'

He stopped, pulled her close again. 'Considering you didn't

run the opposite way when you first saw me, you're still talking to me and you've invited me to dinner, I'm downright ecstatic.'

Joy fizzed in her veins, heady and tingling and making her feel punch-drunk. Sure, they needed to talk but, for now, she was happy too. Happier than she'd been in days. Heck, happier than she'd been in years.

This last week with Ethan, she'd found a surprising peace. She didn't have to pretend to be someone she wasn't, to fake a smile, to be poised and elegant and refined all in the name of appearances.

He saw her for who she was—a woman out to make a new start, a woman happiest with no make-up, no artifice and no platitudes.

'I've never seen you like this.'

He tucked a strand of hair behind her ear, twisting the end around his finger, brushing the delicate skin beneath her ear.

'What? With my hair frizzy from sea water and wearing a kaftan from a local market?'

His gaze searched her face, her eyes, focusing on her lips.

'I've never seen you so relaxed. You're truly happy here, aren't you?'

She nodded, filled with a sense of serenity she'd never had elsewhere.

'Maybe it's a mental thing, knowing my mum spent half her life here and I feel more connected to her here than anywhere.'

'It's more than that.'

He was right. It was the first time in a long time she'd been on her own, content in her own company.

She'd been alone in Melbourne since Richard's death but that had been different. There'd been the whirlwind of the funeral, countless trips to the solicitors, endless paperwork to tidy up and the personal fallout from Richard's little bomb-shell in the form of his girlfriend, Sonja.

Here, there was none of that. She could finally be true to herself, true to *her* needs.

She smiled. 'You've got to know me pretty well, huh?'

'Enough to know I've never seen you so at ease.'

'It's this place.'

She waved at the endless stretch of sand, the shimmering azure sea, the purple-streaked sky scattered with diamond-like stars.

'Not just the tranquillity, the pace of life, but everything about it. I can just be myself, you know.'

'I'm happy for you, Tam, I really am.'

He was, she could see he was genuine, which made her like him all the more.

'But a part of me can't help but wish I'd found you with unwashed hair and chewed-to-the-quick fingernails and pale and sallow from pining away for me, rather than the picture of glowing health.'

She'd pined all right. She'd struggled to sleep the first night, moped around while sightseeing, dragged her feet through this sand on more long walks than she'd ever taken.

Nothing had soothed the hollow ache in her heart, the anxiety gnawing at her belly that she'd lost her chance at exploring something new, something exciting, something that could potentially be the best thing to ever happen to her.

Yet here he was, in the flesh, wearing his trademark rakish pirate smile, khaki shorts and a white T-shirt setting off his newly acquired tan.

He was gorgeous, every tantalising, delectable inch of him, and by coming here, she was hoping he'd made the statement that he was ready to explore this spark between them.

'You're staring.'

She raised an eyebrow, fought a blush. 'Am I?'

'Uh-huh.' He ducked his head for a quick kiss. 'And I like it. That gleam in your beautiful eyes tells me I still have a chance.'

'Only if you're lucky.'

Laughing at his wounded expression, she slipped out of his grasp, hitched up her long skirt and sprinted across the sand with him in hot pursuit.

She'd never felt this carefree, this spontaneous, and while Colva Beach may have worked its magic on her, it had more to do with the man rugby-tackling her to the sand as they reached the hut.

'Hey! Don't go trying out for your Kangaroos footy team by practising on me.'

He rolled onto his back, taking her with him so she lay deliciously along the length of him. 'Wouldn't dream of it. Besides, those guys are way out of my league.'

'Am I?'

All too aware of their heated skin being separated by the sheer chiffon kaftan and cotton, she propped on his chest, the teasing smile dying on her lips as she registered the sudden shadows in his eyes.

'Maybe you are.'

'I was kidding, you great oaf.' She whacked him playfully on the chest, disappointed when he stood and hauled her to her feet.

'Yeah, well, my ego bruises easily. You need to take it easy on me.'

She didn't buy his rueful grin for a second, something akin to hurt still lingering in his eyes.

'I'll keep that in mind.'

Eager to restore the playful mood between them, she gestured to the hut. 'Maybe you won't be so sensitive once you get some food into that great bottomless pit of yours.'

He instantly perked up. 'Did you mention food?'

She laughed, opened the door. 'Kitchen's on the left. Dinner's ready to be heated. I'll just take a quick shower before we eat.'

While she preferred the au naturel look here, she felt distinctly grubby in the presence of his sexy casualness. That glow he'd mentioned probably had more to do with a day's worth of perspiration than any inner peace.

'Right. See you in ten.'

She held up one hand. 'Make that five. I'm starving too.'

Before she could move, he captured her hand, raised it to his lips and placed a hot, scorching kiss on her palm and curled her fingers over. 'I'm really glad I came.'

'Me too,' she murmured, his kiss burning her palm as she kept her hand clenched, backing slowly into the bathroom, not breaking eye contact for a second, waiting until she all but slammed the door before slumping against it in a quivering heap, her hormones leaping as high as her heart.

Ethan headed for the tiny kitchen, drawn by the faintest aroma of fish, onions and ginger.

For a guy who hadn't been able to face food in the last forty-eight hours, he was ravenous.

Not just for food.

The instant he'd laid eyes on Tam, the craving was back, so intense, so overwhelming, he wondered how he'd managed to let her walk away from him in the first place.

All his doubts had washed away on the evening tide as she'd run towards him, her incredible green eyes shining, her smile incandescent.

He wasn't a romantic kind of guy—dating arm-candy women who liked to be seen with rich guys took all the gloss off romance—but, if he were prone to it, he'd say their reunion had been picture perfect, the type of moment to relate to their kids, their grandkids.

Whoa!

He stopped dead, backing up a moment.

He'd gone from the possibility of dating to kids?

This hunger must be making him more light-headed than

he'd first thought and, heading for the fridge, he dug out a casserole dish filled with fish curry, a bowl of steamed white rice and a raita made from yoghurt, cucumber, tomato and onion.

Food of the gods, he thought, smiling to himself as he heated the fish and rice, amazed he'd gone a whole day without thinking of his precious Ambrosia.

He spent all day every day in constant touch with the managers of each restaurant around the world, keeping abreast of the daily running, meeting with accountants, conference calling with staff.

Being in control of Ambrosia, seeing his business grow to international stardom status never failed to give him a kick, a solid reminder of how far he'd come.

From loitering around the back door of Ma Petite, hoping for food scraps, to being taken under the wing of the great Arnaud Fournier and given an apprenticeship in his world-class restaurant, to working eighty-hour weeks and scrounging every cent to invest in his first restaurant, to running one of the most famous restaurant chains in the world was heady stuff for a guy who could still remember the pinch of hunger in his belly and the dirt under his fingernails from scrabbling for the last stale bun out of a dumpster.

From bum to billionaire and he couldn't be prouder.

Then why hadn't he told Tam the truth?

They'd discussed her family, her career, but he'd neatly sidestepped any personal questions she'd aimed his way, reluctant to taint her image of him.

Why? Was he ashamed? Embarrassed? Afraid she'd see him as less of a man?

Hell, yeah. The less said about his sordid past the better. She was taking a huge step forward, both career-wise and personally, in letting him get close and he'd be a fool to risk it by giving her a glimpse into the real him.

'Something smells good.'

She stepped into the kitchen, her hair wet and slicked back into a low ponytail, her skin clear and glowing, wearing a simple red sundress with tiny white polka dots, and he slammed the hot rice dish onto the bench top before the whole thing slid onto the floor courtesy of his fumbling fingers.

She had that effect on him, could render him useless and floundering out of his depth with a smile, with a single glance from beneath those long dark lashes that accentuated the unique green of her eyes.

'Now who's staring?'

She sashayed across the kitchen, lifted the lid on the fish and waved the fragrant aroma towards her nose. 'Wait until you try this fish moilee. It's fabulous.'

Thankful she'd given him a chance to unglue his tongue from the roof of his mouth where it had stuck the moment he'd caught sight of her, he quickly set the table.

'How's moilee different from curry?'

'Different spices, different method of cooking.' She gathered a jug of mango lassi, a delicious yoghurt and fruit drink he loved, and glasses and placed them on the table. 'You add a little salt and lime juice to the fish, set it aside for a while. Then you fry mustard seeds, curry leaves, onion, ginger, garlic, green chillies and turmeric before adding the fish, covering the lot with coconut milk and letting it simmer.'

She inhaled again, closed her eyes, her expression ecstatic and he cleared his throat, imagining what else, apart from a tasty curry, could bring that look to her face.

'My mouth's watering. Let's eat.'

Her eyes snapped open at his abrupt response and he busied himself with transporting the hot dishes to the table under her speculative stare rather than have to explain why he was losing his cool.

For a couple who'd chatted amicably during most meals on their Palace on Wheels journey, they were strangely silent as they devoured the delicious fish and rice, darting occasional glances at each other over the lassi, politely passing the raita, focusing on forking food into their mouths.

Tension stretched between them, taut and fraught, as he wished he could articulate half of what he was feeling. Overwhelmed. Out of control. And more attracted to anyone than he'd been in his entire life.

He'd dated many women, most had left him cold. He told himself he liked it that way; he chose fickle women because he didn't want to get emotionally involved.

So what was he doing here, now, hoping this incredible woman would let him into her heart when he knew that would be an irrevocable step down a very dangerous road, a road less travelled for him, a road peppered with emotions he'd rather ignore?

Tam had been grieving, had closed down emotionally, hadn't dated, let alone looked at a guy since Rich's death.

Yet here she was, opening her heart to him, welcoming him back despite how he'd acted like a jerk, first on the train, then in Udaipur, lastly in Delhi. Which could only mean one thing.

She was already emotionally involved with him, was willing to gamble her heart on him.

He had no idea if he deserved it.

'That was delish.' She patted her mouth with a napkin, refolded it, before sitting back and rubbing her tummy. 'I don't think I could move for a week after that, which gives you plenty of time to start talking.'

So much for being let off the hook. She'd lulled him into a false sense of security, yet he'd known it would come to this.

He had to tell her the truth—some of it—if they were to have any chance of moving forward from here.

Wishing he hadn't eaten so much—it now sat like a lump of lead in his gut—he sat back, crossed his ankles, wondering if she'd buy his relaxed posture while inside he churned with trepidation.

Opening up to anyone, let alone the woman he cared about, didn't sit well with him and he'd be damned if he messed this up after what had happened in Delhi.

Folding his arms, he looked her straight in the eye. 'You want to know why I backed off at India Gate.'

'For starters.'

She didn't look angry—far from it if the gentle upturning of her lips was any indication. Yet she had every right to be, every right to kick his sorry butt out of here after the way he'd treated her.

'Did you ever want something so badly as a kid, something you wished for, something that consumed you yet, when you got it, you didn't know what to do with it?'

Understanding turned her eyes verdigris. 'I was a bit like that with my Baby Born doll. Really wanted one, then when I got it for Christmas, didn't know whether I should feed it or burp it or change its nappy first.'

'You're laughing at me.'

'I'm not.'

Her twitching mouth made a mockery of her last statement and he chuckled, shook his head.

'I'll be honest with you, Tam. I came on this trip because I wanted you. Then I started to get to know you—really know you—and it's like…'

How could he explain it? Like being hit over the head with a four-by-two? Like being struck by lightning? Like having the blinkers ripped from his eyes only to see the stunning, vibrant woman he desired was so much more than he could've possibly imagined?

'It's like…?'

Her soft prompt had him saying the first thing that popped into his head.

'It's like finding the person you want most in this world is holding the key to your heart as well.'

No way—had he really said that?

Inwardly cringing at his emotional explosion, he met her gaze, the shimmer of tears in her eyes slugging him harder than the realisation that this had already moved beyond caring for him, that he was already half in love with her.

'Look, that's too heavy—'

'Don't you dare apologise for saying that!' Her head snapped up, her gaze defiant as the tears spilled over and rolled down her cheeks. 'Do you have any idea how I feel, hearing you say that?'

'Like bolting?' he ventured, earning another wide-eyed stare.

'Like this.'

She stood so abruptly her chair slammed onto the floor and she traversed the tiny table in a second, flinging herself onto his lap and wrapping her arms tightly around his neck.

'Well, now, maybe I should blurt my innermost thoughts more often if this is the type of reaction I get.'

Her eyes gleamed with mischief. 'No, *this* is the type of reaction you get.'

She covered his mouth with hers in a desperate, frantic kiss filled with longing and passion and recklessness.

The type of kiss that filled his heart with hope, the type of kiss with the power to teach him this relinquishing control lark wasn't half as scary as he'd built it up to be.

She was warm and vibrant and responsive in his arms, her hunger matching his and, as she shifted in his lap, inflaming him further, he knew he had to put a stop to this before they jumped way ahead of themselves.

He wasn't a Boy Scout and he'd like nothing better than to carry her into the bedroom right this very second and make love to her all night long but he'd botched things with her once; he'd be damned if he made another mistake now.

And that was what sex would be, despite the blood pounding through his body and urging him to follow through—a mistake.

He wanted to take things slow this time. He'd rushed her on the train journey, had almost lost her because of it, and there was no way in Hades he'd make the same mistake twice.

'Tam?'

'Hmm?'

She nuzzled his neck, giving his good intentions a thorough hiding as she straddled him, her breasts pushing deliciously against his chest.

'I can't stay.'

She stilled, raised her head, her eyes glazed, confused. 'Why not?'

Cradling her face in his hands, he brushed a soft kiss across her swollen lips.

'Because I want to do this right.'

He didn't have to add *this time*.

He saw the respect in her eyes, the understanding, and knowing this incredible woman was on the same wavelength as him sent another flood of intense longing washing over him.

'Great, the playboy has morphed into a goody two shoes,' she said, sliding off his lap in a slow, deliberate movement designed to tease as he clenched his hands to stop himself from reaching out and yanking her back down.

'Oh, you'll see how good I really am.'

He stood, pulling her back into his arms, enjoying her squeal of pure delight. 'Soon—very soon.'

'I'll hold you to that.'

'I'm counting on it.'

This time their kiss was slower, exploratory, leisurely, and as he reluctantly slipped out of her arms and raised his hand in goodbye he feared there'd come a time in the not too distant future where he'd find it near on impossible to walk away from her.

CHAPTER ELEVEN

'I THOUGHT Goa was settled by the Portuguese?'

Tamara nodded, browsing the market stall's brightly coloured powders for the Holi festival tomorrow. 'It was. That's why you see so many Portuguese-inspired buildings and a lot of the population are Catholic. Apparently thousands of people make the pilgrimage to see Saint Francis Xavier's body at the basilica here every five years.'

Ethan trailed his fingers through a mound of sunshine-yellow powder and earned a frown from the vendor for his trouble.

'If it's predominantly Catholic, what's with this Holi festival? Isn't that Hindu?'

'Uh-huh. But, like most of India, there are so many different religions and castes living side by side that everyone's pretty tolerant of the different festivals.' She pointed to several piles of powder, smiling at the vendor, who began shovelling mini mountains of the stuff into clear plastic bags. 'I think it's fabulous everyone gets involved. It's such a joyous occasion that you can't help but get swept up in the fun. At least, that's what Mum told me.'

He nodded, pointing to the bags being thrust into her hands. 'So tell me about it. All I know is everyone goes berserk and throws colour on everyone else.'

Upon hearing this, the vendor frowned again and shook his

head, while she handed him rupees and laughed. 'Come on, I'll enlighten you over a cup of masala chai.'

'Sounds good.'

He held out his hand for her carry-all and she gratefully gave it to him. Choosing every colour of the rainbow for Holi mightn't be such a great idea if she had to lug all those kilos back to the hut.

'Do the colours mean anything?'

She nodded, instantly transported back to the first time she'd heard about Holi, sitting on her mum's knee. She'd just learned to make her first chapatti that same day, and had had so much fun rolling the balls of dough into flat breads, standing on a stool next to the stove as her mum had fried them.

She'd been five at the time and her dad had come home after work, scoffed three with jam and pronounced them better than her mum's.

It'd been a magical day, one of those days where her mum was reminiscing about India, eager to tell stories, and she'd lapped it up. Yet another thing she missed.

'Green's for vitality, red is purity, blue is calmness and yellow is piety.'

He squinted through the bag. 'So what happens when you mix the lot together?'

'You'll find out.'

She could hardly wait. Ever since she'd first learned of the festival of colour, she'd been entranced. The freedom to play and dance and sing like a kid, flinging coloured powders and water balloons over anyone and everyone, visiting friends, exchanging gifts and sweets, all sounded like a good time.

'Let's have a cuppa here.'

They stopped at a roadside café, ordered masala chais and relaxed, watching the passing procession of people gearing up for Holi, each weighed down with vibrant magentas, daffodil-yellows, peacock-blues, dazzling emeralds and vivid crimsons.

Ethan gestured towards the passing parade. 'Looks like everyone gets in on the act.'

She nodded, delighting in the infectious excitement of the kids bouncing down the street, laden down with colour-filled bags.

'It's a time where age is irrelevant; everyone joins in. You can get wild and no one will blink.'

It was also a time for lovers, where the application of colour to each other was a sign of their love. Wisely, she kept that gem to herself. It was hard enough handling the swift shift in their relationship, and trying not to dwell on the erotic dreams of the last few nights, without adding to it.

He leaned forward, crooked his finger at her. 'How wild?'

She laughed. 'It's good clean fun. Well, if you discount getting dirty with colours, that is.'

His devilish grin sent heat sizzling through her. 'I'm all for getting dirty.'

'I bet.'

Her dry response had him chuckling as the waiter deposited two stainless-steel mugs filled to the brim with steaming chai in front of them.

'So what does it all mean?'

'There are loads of different legends surrounding it, centring on the ultimate victory of good over evil. Holi helps people believe in the virtue of being honest and banishing evil. It helps bring the country together and the tradition is that even enemies turn into friends during the festival.'

She sipped at her chai, sighing as the burst of cardamom-flavoured tea hit her taste buds. 'And there's no differentiation between rich and poor. Everyone gets in on the fun. It's about strengthening bonds between friends, revitalising relationships.'

'Wow, sounds like the world could do with a good Holi festival every now and then.'

She nodded. 'Wouldn't it be great? A sea of colour and a giant group hug.'

'I could do with a hug myself.' He stared at her over the rim of his mug, his blue eyes mischievous. 'Similar to that one you gave me at your kitchen table the night I arrived.'

She blushed, tried a frown and failed miserably when her lips curved into a secretive smile at the memory.

'Drink your chai. We have about half an hour to get changed before the fun starts.'

'Make that five minutes if we get back to the hut in time.'

She almost choked on her tea. He hadn't flirted so blatantly since he'd arrived, hadn't pushed, despite the increasingly heated kisses they'd shared the last few days.

He wanted to take things slow and while her head and heart were grateful for the fact, her body was way behind in the acceptance stakes.

Something had shifted today. Ever since he'd turned up on her doorstep this morning and all through their stroll around the market he'd been pushing the boundaries, flirting outrageously, hinting at something more than a quick, sizzling kiss at the end of the day.

She'd put it down to infectious Holi madness. Who knew— maybe, just maybe, there would be some revitalising of their relationship happening later tonight?

'This is insane!' Ethan shouted at the top of his lungs, dodging another kid pointing a super-sized water soaker at him, bright blue this time, only to be splattered in the middle of the back by a magenta water bomb from Tam.

'Yeah, isn't it great?' She flung her arms overhead, twirled around, did a defiant jig in front of him, taunting him now he'd used up his colour supplies.

He advanced towards her, pointing at the remaining bags in her hand. 'Give me some of that.'

'No.' She stood on tiptoe, jiggled the bags in front of him. 'Not my fault your aim is lousy.'

'That does it!' He grabbed her around the waist and she squealed, her laughter firing his blood as much as having her wriggling and warm and vibrant in his arms. 'Tam, I'm warning you—'

'You're in no position to warn me. I'm the one holding the ammunition.'

To reinforce the point, she swung one of the bags at his back, where it exploded, drenching him further.

'What colour was that?'

'Red, to match your face for letting a girl beat you at this.'

'That does it.' He hoisted her over his shoulder, growling when she emptied the last few bags on his back, then proceeded to pummel him with her fists.

'Put me down.'

He patted her butt in response. 'Nope, sorry, no can do. This is Holi, remember? Anything goes.'

'I take it back.'

'Too late.'

She stiffened as he slid a hand up her calf, reaching her thigh, all in the name of getting a better grip. That was his excuse and he was sticking to it.

'Are you copping a cheap feel?'

'No, just don't want to drop you and ruin your outfit.'

'But it's already ruined—'

'Gotcha!'

She pummelled harder, he laughed harder and he jogged the last few metres to her hut, deliberately sliding her down nice and slow, her body deliciously rubbing against his.

This was madness—pure and utter madness.

So much for taking things slow.

Every moment he spent in Tam's company, he found it harder to resist her, harder not to say caution be damned and sweep her into his arms and make slow, passionate love to her all night long.

He wanted her. Thoughts of her consumed him every waking moment and most sleeping ones too and now, with her standing less than a foot away, her tie-dyed kaftan plastered to her curvy body, he knew he couldn't hold out much longer.

He wanted to do the right thing, give her time to adjust to their new relationship but his knight in shining armour routine had taken a serious beating since he'd arrived on her doorstep earlier that week and she'd welcomed him with open arms.

'So?'

'So…' His gaze dipped, took in her orange, green and blue spattered face, her purple matted hair and the Technicolor kaftan.

Despite the mess, she'd never looked so beautiful and he clenched his hands to stop himself from reaching out to her and never letting go.

'Time to clean up.' She stepped back, as if sensing his urge. 'Though some of us need more cleaning up than others.'

She pointed to his irredeemable T-shirt. 'Not only can some of us not throw, we're none too crash hot at dodging too.'

'You're asking for it.'

He made a grab for her and they tumbled through the doorway, drenched to the skin and laughing uncontrollably.

'You look like a preschooler's finger-painting.'

'You look worse.'

They stared at each other and laughed again, as Tamara clutched her side. 'I'm sore.'

'From taking my direct hits full on?'

'More like from dodging your average throws.'

He pointed to her powder-spattered kaftan. 'Then how do you explain all that colour?'

She shrugged, put a thumb up to her nose and waggled her fingers. 'Other people.'

He advanced towards her. 'Are you saying my aim is lousy?'

She smiled. 'Oh, yeah. Though you might've landed a few lucky shots. Beginner's luck and all that.'

'Beginner, huh?' He continued to advance, his mouth twitching, his eyes filled with devilry and she backed up, stumbling into the bathroom. 'You going to admit I'm good?'

He halted less than two feet in front of her, close enough to feel his radiant heat, not close enough according to her body, straining towards him.

Tilting her chin up, she tossed her bedraggled hair over a shoulder. 'Never.'

'Never's a long time, sweetheart.'

His hand shot out, captured her wrist, tugging her closer and she laughed when their bodies made a strange squelching sound as they came into contact.

'Ready to concede?'

'Nope.' She shook her head, spraying them with the finest purple droplets, like sparkling amethysts raining from a jewelled sky.

'Well, then, I might just have to make you.'

His eyes glittered with pure devilry as he lowered his head, brushed his mouth across hers in a slow, masterful kiss that had her clinging to his wet T-shirt, her knees wobbling.

'Concede?'

Her tongue darted out to moisten her lips, still tingling from his kiss. 'I think I need more convincing.'

He growled, swept her up in his arms and deposited her on the hand basin, the hard, cold enamel barely registering as he swooped in for another kiss, a fiery, passionate explosion of melding mouths that heated her from the inside out and would've dried her clothes if they'd continued.

But she stopped, uncurled her fingers from where they clung to his T-shirt, all too aware of where this would lead.

'What's wrong?'

How could she articulate half of what she was feeling?

Blinding anticipation at being touched by a man after so long?

Good old-fashioned lust that licked along her veins and made her throb with need?

Crippling uncertainty that she wouldn't live up to his expectations?

Or the mind-numbing fear that, once she took this irreversible step, there'd be no going back?

Making love with Ethan would be just that for her—making love—and it would cement what she'd known the last few days.

She'd fallen in love with him.

Enough to take a chance on love again, enough to want it all—with him.

'Tam?'

He tipped up her chin, leaving her no option but to stare into his glittering blue eyes, those eyes she'd seen clear and sincere, determined and focused at work, currently a smoky gentian with passion.

'I'm scared.'

He cupped her cheek, drawing comforting circles in the small of her back with his other hand. 'I'd never do anything to hurt you.'

'I know, but—'

'But?'

'What if—' *this doesn't work, this makes you pull back again, this makes me fall in love with you even more and you don't feel half as much for me as I feel for you?*

'What if you stop second-guessing this and let me love you?'

She knew he meant it as a physical expression of love, but hearing him say the word out loud banished the last of her lingering doubts.

She'd spent every moment of her marriage carefully weighing and assessing—trying to say the right thing, do the right thing, wear the right thing. And she'd been miserable.

Now she had a second chance, a real chance at happiness and she'd be a fool to let it slip through her fingers.

Her hands slid up his chest, caressed his neck, cradled his face as she wrapped her legs around him. 'What if I show you how much I want this?'

His face creased into an instant smile, the heartrendingly familiar sexy smile that never failed to set her pulse racing.

'Sounds like a plan.'

He sent a pointed glance at their clothes. 'But we're filthy.'

Shocked at her bravado, she met his gaze head-on.

'Let's take a shower, then.'

His eyes, radiating enough heat to scorch her clothes right off her, never left hers as she reached out, her fingers grappling with the hem of his wet T-shirt before peeling it upwards with slow, exquisite deliberation, revealing inch by inch of spectacular hard, bronzed chest.

When she reached his shoulders, he helped shrug it off, leaving his torso deliciously bare, beckoning her fingertips to explore.

And explore she did, smoothing her palms over every hard plane, skating her fingertips over every ridge, every delineation, her breath catching as his hands shot out and captured her wrists.

'My turn,' he gritted out, ducking for a searing kiss before almost tearing her kaftan off. 'I've waited too long for this to take it slow.'

'Fast is good,' she gasped as, with a deft flick of the clasp on her bra, he had her breasts spilling free into his waiting hands.

'Ethan…'

She whispered his name on a sigh, a long, drawn-out, blissful sigh as his mouth replaced his hands until she almost passed out from the blinding intensity.

'You're so beautiful, so responsive,' he murmured, kissing his way down her body as sensation after sensation slammed into her, rendering a simple task like standing impossible.

She sagged against the basin, braced her hands on it as his fingers hovered, toyed with the elastic of her panties.

'I want this to be beyond special for you,' he said, wrenching a low moan from deep within as he set about doing just that.

She'd never been loved like this, never had a man want to please her first, please her so totally before taking his satisfaction and as Ethan brought her to the peak of ecstasy and she tumbled over the edge into an explosion of mind-numbing bliss, she finally came alive.

When he stood, she cradled his face, stared into his eyes, hoping he could read the depth of emotion there.

'Thank you,' she said, gasping as he pressed against her, her desire needing little to reignite.

'The pleasure's all mine.'

His roguish smile brought out the pirate in him and she gladly wrapped her arms around his waist, more than happy to be ravaged.

As the steam rose around them, she lost all sense of time. His shorts joined her discarded clothes, his body melded with hers and he made passionate love to her until she almost cried with the beauty of it.

Later, as he held her close, cocooned in the safety of his arms, the heat from their bodies drying them better than any towels, she knew without a doubt that this man was her destiny.

Ethan groaned, sat back and patted his stomach. 'Okay, now I'm done, are you going to tell me what's in that sorpotel?'

The corners of Tam's mouth twitched, the tiny movement slugging him as he recalled in vivid detail how those lips had explored his body last night. He'd dated widely but never had he felt so connected with a woman in the bedroom.

Though it was more than that and he knew it—knew it with every guarded cell in his body. What he felt for Tam defied description and had him jumpier than a mongoose around a cobra.

If she'd zapped his control before, he didn't stand a chance now; he wanted her more than ever. It was like sampling the finest Shiraz Grenache: one taste was never enough.

'You sure you want to know?'

He pointed to the empty bowl, where he'd mopped up every last bit of gravy with a paratha. 'Considering I've just devoured the richest curry I've ever had without leaving a drop, I think I can handle it.'

'It's made from pork, beef and pig's blood.'

Ignoring the smallest tumble of revolt his belly gave, he reached for his coconut milk and raised it to her.

'Nothing like those magic secret ingredients.'

She leaned across the table, giving him a delectable view of her cleavage and, to his credit, he managed to keep his gaze on her face.

'You don't have to pretend with me.'

His belly griped again but this time it had nothing to do with the thought of eating pig's blood.

He *was* pretending with her, living a fantasy—one he'd craved a long time. But fantasies didn't mesh with reality and if there was one thing he'd come to respect, it was reality.

He lived the reality every day—of trusting no one but himself, of staying on top in business, of never losing control.

Yet here, now, with Tam staring at him with a new sparkle in her eyes and a permanent smile on her face, he wasn't just in danger of losing control. He was in danger of losing his mind.

Seeing curiosity creep into her gaze, he clanked his coconut against hers. 'I couldn't come to a Goan institution like Souza Lobo's and not try the sorpotel. So, whatever's next, bring it on.'

Her eyes twinkled as she lowered her coconut. 'Brave words from a guy who got obliterated during Holi.'

He shrugged, thankful they'd safely navigated back to playful. 'I just wanted you to think you had the upper hand.'

'Didn't I?'

'I'll let you in on a little secret.'

He crooked his finger at her, laughing when she twisted it. 'I was lulling you into a false sense of security.'

The twinkle faded, replaced by a flicker of fear that had him cursing his poor choice of words.

Of course she'd be insecure with how fast things had developed between them. In effect, he was her rebound guy, the first guy she'd allowed near her after the love of her life, and having her questioning whether it was the right thing to do was a dumb move, however inadvertent.

Placing a finger under her chin, he tipped it up. 'I'm kidding.'

'I know.'

But he'd shattered the light-hearted mood and, considering he had no idea how to deal with emotion, was having a damn hard time getting it back.

'I know.' He snapped his fingers. 'Let's go haggle for some of those handmade Kashmiri scarves you were admiring on the way over here.'

Her mouth twisted in a wry grin. 'That's the second time this trip you've tried to distract me with the inducement of shopping.'

'Is it working?'

'I'll let you know when you've bought me a scarf or two.'

Happy to have the smile back on her face, he held out his hand. 'Me?'

'Yeah, don't you tycoons like flashing your cash around?'

'Only to impress.'

'Well, I'm ready to be impressed. Lead the way.'

As she slipped her hand into his, it hit him how truly lucky he was.

Despite her joking around, Tam wasn't remotely interested in his money. With the type of women he usually dated that meant a lot to him, but here, with the pungent aromas of frying spices and fresh seafood in the air, the hot sand squelching between his toes and the relentless sun beating down, it merely added to the unreality of the situation.

He was in a tropical hot spot with a gorgeous woman, they'd become lovers and grown closer than he'd dared imagine.

Was any of this real?

Would it evaporate as quickly as the steam off flavoursome mulligatawny when they returned to Melbourne? Did he want it to?

He liked Tam—a lot. But did he like her enough to give up the habits of a lifetime and relinquish control of his tightly held emotions?

'Come on, I see a flea market over there with my name written on a few dozen scarves.'

He groaned, delighting in her wide grin while trying to hide his inner turmoil.

Tamara leaned back against Ethan, secure in the circle of his arms. These days, there was no place she'd rather be.

'Comfortable?'

Turning her face up, her breath caught at the beauty of his face, shadows from the fire flickering over his cheekbones, highlighting his strong nose, the curve of his lips.

He was gorgeous and, for now, he was hers.

'Very.'

She wriggled back slightly, enjoying the sudden flare of heat in his eyes, the wickedly sexy smile.

'When you first mentioned a full moon party at Arjuna Beach, I envisaged a bunch of hippies drinking and having a full-on rave complete with bubbles. Nothing like this.'

He cuddled her closer, sweeping a kiss across her lips before resting his chin on her shoulder, content to just hold her as they stared at the bonfire one of the revellers had lit not far from the water's edge.

The stubble peppering his jaw brushed her cheek, the tiny

prickles strangely comforting. Gone was the slick, smooth, clean-shaven corporate pirate; in his place was his laid-back, easygoing, constantly smiling counterpart.

And she liked this guy much better.

How had she ever thought him distant and ruthless and aloof? The Ethan she'd got to know the last two weeks, the Ethan she'd fallen for, was warm and spontaneous and generous. He made her laugh, made her forget every sane reason why she shouldn't be losing her heart to him.

But what if it was too late? For, no matter how attentive and carefree he was here, she knew once they returned to Melbourne he'd revert back to type and she'd be left with nothing but memories.

She'd known it from the start, had held him at bay because of it, but no amount of self-talk could withstand a barrage of Ethan at his best: charming, gregarious and able to make her feel one hundred per cent female.

That was most seductive of all, for she hadn't felt this way in a long, long time.

Not only had Richard sapped her identity, he'd battered her self-esteem and, thanks to Ethan, she'd rediscovered another part of herself she'd thought lost—she was still a desirable woman, capable of instilling passion in a man and, right now, that made her feel like a million dollars.

'You've heard pretty much anything goes at these full moon parties, right?'

'Yeah.' His soft breath caressed her ear, sending a shiver of delight through her. 'So what do you have in mind?'

Tilting her face up to see him, she said, 'Dance with me.'

'Here?'

His dubious glance flicked to the couples surrounding the fire, some of them entwined, some holding hands, some lying back and staring at the stars, and she laughed at his doubtful expression.

'I love dancing and haven't done it for ages.'

His reticence melted away at her wistful tone and he stood, tugging her to her feet in one fluid movement, pulling her close until her breasts were squashed against his chest and her pelvis snuggled in his.

'How's that?'

'Perfect.'

And it was, not just the way their bodies fitted but the way he held her, as if she was something precious, something he never wanted to let go.

While logic said she was kidding herself in thinking that even for a second, her heart was going with the flow, caught up in the magic of the moment with soft sand still warm from the day's sun under her feet, Ethan's sandalwood scent enveloping her and his body speaking to her on some subconscious level.

They didn't speak, her head resting on his shoulder as they swayed in time to the sultry strains of a sitar, the drugging beat of a tabla. Closing her eyes, everything faded: the other couples, the fire, the music, the waves lapping at the water's edge.

She wanted to remember every second of tonight, imprint every incredible moment in her memory, for this was the night.

The night she admitted she'd fallen in love.

While she might not be ready to admit it to Ethan yet, the knowledge that she'd come so far—opening her heart again, learning to trust, taking a chance—was beyond empowering.

As the sitar faded, Ethan pulled away and she looked up, wondering if he could read the exultation in her eyes.

Cupping her cheek, he said, 'You're glowing.'

Smiling, she stood on tiptoe and kissed him. 'Thanks to you.'

'So I'm forgiven for muscling in on your holiday? And for deliberately making us miss the train in Udaipur?'

'Why, you—'

She whacked him on the chest and he laughed, swooping

in for a quick kiss. 'I had this stupid notion you'd fall for me surrounded by all that romance.'

'I don't need all those trappings.'

Sliding her arms around his waist, she snuggled into him again. 'You've kind of grown on me.'

'Good. You know why?'

'Why?'

'Because we only have a few days left and I intend to spend every second by your side. Think you can handle that?'

Ignoring the flutter of panic at the thought of what they had ending in a few days, she nodded. 'Yeah.'

'Then what are we waiting for? Let's head back and start making the most of our time together.'

His mouth captured hers again, his kiss searing as she melted against him, powerless to do anything other than want him, no matter how much her inner voice warned her their time together would soon be coming to an end.

'You sure you don't want me to come with you? I can always postpone this meeting.'

Tamara waved Ethan away. 'Go take care of your business. I'll meet you back at the hut later.'

'Not too much later.'

He pulled her in for a swift scorching kiss that sizzled all the way to her toes, leaving her breathless as he winked and waved, heading for the nearest five star hotel.

She watched him until he was a tiny speck in the distance, a tall figure striding down the dusty road with the long, determined steps of a man with things to do, places to be.

But he wasn't running from her and that was a bonus—a big one.

Since they'd made love two nights ago, they'd spent every waking moment together. All the things she'd planned on doing, like eating at Souza Lobo's and attending a full moon party, had been much more special with Ethan by her side, sharing the experience.

As for the nights…exploring each other's bodies, pleasuring each other…had surpassed any expectations she'd ever had.

Richard had been selfish so it figured he'd been a selfish lover too. But Ethan… Just thinking about the ways he gave her joy brought a blush to her cheeks.

Their time together had been beyond special. They were good together—really good. You couldn't fake what they had.

An unexpected chill ran down her spine as she remembered how she'd faked a lot during her marriage, how easy it was to act one way while feeling another.

Ethan may be a player but surely he didn't treat all his women this way? Surely his actions spoke louder than words in the way he'd cherished her in Goa?

While she hadn't gone into this expecting him to love her, now she'd fallen for him she couldn't help but wish they could explore this further.

He'd barrelled into her life when she'd least expected or wanted it but, now he was here, she hoped he'd stay.

She stopped in front of a sari shop, pressed her hands to the dusty glass and peered inside. Her mum had always wanted her to wear a sari, just once, but she'd never had the occasion or the inclination. Besides, Richard would've had a fit if she'd paraded her ethnicity around in front of his posh friends.

She'd overheard him once, boasting about her royal heritage or some such guff, implying she descended from a line of exotic East Indian princesses. She'd confronted him later and in typical fashion he'd laughed off her concerns, saying he had standards to live up to in the public eye and people liked that sort of thing.

She hadn't, though. She'd hated it and, while she'd toed the line in the vain hope of making her marriage work, the lies he'd told had never sat well with her.

Lies far more poisonous and extending further than she'd ever thought possible, considering what had come to light after his death.

Making an impulsive decision to buy one more souvenir of her memorable time here, she pushed open the door and stepped into the welcome coolness of the shop.

'*Namaste.* Can I help you, madam?'

The older woman placed her palms together and gave a little bow, her sightless eyes honing in on Tamara with unerring accuracy as she wondered how a blind woman could assist customers in a shop filled with so much vibrant colour.

'Yes, thanks, I'm looking for a sari.'

Duh! Not unlikely, considering she'd entered a sari shop.

'Anything in particular?'

She shook her head, belatedly realising the woman couldn't see her. 'I've never worn a sari before.'

'But it is in your blood.'

Her eyebrows rose at that. How could the woman know her background? Even if she could see, her light olive skin, green eyes and black hair could be any nationality.

'You are after something like this.'

It was a statement rather than a question as the woman ran her hands along countless silk, chiffon saris until she hovered over one, in the palest of mint-greens.

Her breath caught as the woman held it up, the exquisite length of material catching the sunlight filtering through the front window, the sari shimmering like the iced peppermint milkshakes she'd loved as a kid.

It was perfect, something she'd never imagine wearing; yet, with the shop filled with so many dazzling combinations, she should have a look around rather than grab the first thing on offer. Probably the most expensive sari in the shop and the woman thought she'd be foolish enough to pounce on it.

'Actually, I'm not sure what I want.'

The sari slid through the woman's fingers like quicksilver as she turned her head towards her.

'I think you do.'

A ripple of unease puckered her skin as she registered the woman wasn't talking about the sari.

She knew India was a country big on legends and myths and superstitions. Her mum had told her many stories of ghosts and ghoulies and mysterious happenings but, as far as she was concerned, her superstitious nature extended to a quick glance at the daily horoscope in the morning newspaper, and only then for a laugh.

But here, now, standing in this ancient shop, the heady fragrance of neroli and saffron in the air, surrounded by the soft swish of silk as the woman continued to run her hands over the saris, she could almost believe there was something 'otherworldly' at play.

'The sari is beautiful but—'

'You are searching. For many things. For love. For a home. For yourself.'

Another shiver ran through her. Okay, this was getting too spooky.

The woman was scarily accurate, though her predictions had been pretty generic. What tourist wouldn't be on a quest, searching for something, if only a good time?

'You have love. But all is not as it seems.'

She'd got that right. Since when was anything in her life simple?

'You will face many obstacles on your path to true happiness.'

More generic stuff and she'd had enough.

'Actually, that sari's perfect.' Checking out the price tag, she sagged with relief. 'I'll take it.'

She thrust money towards the woman, somewhat chastened when she shook her head, sadness creasing her face.

Great, she'd offended the soothsayer. Who knew what fortune she'd get now?

'You will face trials, recross oceans, to find true happiness.'

Giving the woman money and all but yanking her purchase out of her hands hadn't stopped the predications so she'd better make a run for it.

'Thank you.'

She had her hand on the door handle, eager to leave, when the woman stopped her with a low groan that raised the hackles on her neck.

'Take care, my dear. You will need to be on the lookout for false happiness.'

Okay, enough was enough.

She bolted from the shop, wishing she could outrun her doubts as fast as the blind woman. As if she wasn't filled with qualms already, she had some crazy fortune-teller fuelling her insecurities.

This was why she didn't pay attention to superstitious nonsense. Yet, no matter how hard she tried to forget the woman's predictions on the walk back to the hut, she couldn't help but feel she'd voiced some of her own concerns.

Was her relationship with Ethan too good to be true?

Was it all just a mirage, a *false happiness* that would fall down around her ears once they returned to Melbourne?

She'd talked herself into believing what they had was real. She was good at that. Convincing herself to see things in a positive light, no matter how dire they were. She was an expert considering she'd done it for most of her marriage.

There was a huge difference between faking happiness and experiencing the real thing and, while this last week with Ethan had shown her the difference, she still couldn't banish her doubts.

She'd come so far. Over the past year she would've wallowed in them, let them drag her down. Not now. Taking this trip had not only boosted her esteem, fuelled her confidence and encouraged her to take risks she'd never thought possible, she'd also become an optimist. Looking on the bright side was much more liberating than brooding and, for now, she'd take each day as it came with Ethan.

As for what happened in Melbourne, she'd find out soon enough. They were due to fly back tomorrow.

Back to the real world. Back to a new life for her. She had a new job to find, apartment-hunting and a new beginning with Ethan.

Ethan, the man she'd fallen in love with against her will. Her friend, her lover, her soulmate.

Her mum had been right. Every person had a soulmate and she'd just taken a detour on the way to finding hers.

They could have a future together—a good one.

This time, she wouldn't settle for anything less.

CHAPTER TWELVE

'LET me guess. You have business to take care of.'

Ethan leaned over, brushed a kiss across her lips. 'You know me too well.'

'I do now.'

Tamara placed a possessive hand on his arm, scraped her fingernails lightly across the skin, enjoying his slight shudder before he clamped his hand over hers, blatant hunger in his eyes.

'I promise I'll make it the fastest investors meeting on record.' He glanced at his watch, grimaced. 'I have to run. How about I meet you at Ambrosia afterwards?'

'Only if you make me a hot chocolate.'

'Over your chai addiction already?'

'No, but I remember that fabulous hot chocolate you made the day you came back and have a real hankering for it.'

He paused, his expression inscrutable and for a split second a finger of unease strummed her spine. 'So much has changed since that day.'

'For the better.'

He nodded, his tight-lipped expression not inspiring her with confidence. 'I've been doing a bit of thinking.'

The shiver increased. 'About?'

'About making up for lost time. About how much time I wasted not being around this last year, not seducing you earlier.'

That surprised her. She'd been anticipating many responses but not that one.

'Maybe I wasn't ready to be seduced?'

He smiled at her hand-on-out-thrust-hip defiance. 'Lucky for me you are now.'

'You think you've got me wrapped around your perfect little finger, huh?'

'Hey, I'm not perfect. Pretty tarnished, in fact.'

'Not to me.'

She wound her arms around his neck, snuggled close, breathing in his fresh, just-showered scent, wishing he didn't have to dash off.

They'd barely been back in the country six hours and it was business as usual for him. Not that it surprised her. His dynamic go-get-'em attitude was one of the things she loved about him.

While Richard had been good at his job—the best according to the experts—Ethan had a quiet confidence underlined by success.

She'd once been good at her job too, before she'd given it all up for Richard, and she couldn't wait to get back to it.

The restaurateur and the food critic.

People would talk, would say she'd moved on from the chef to the owner, but let them. She'd faced the media barrage after Richard died and, while she'd hated every minute at the time, she'd weathered the storm.

She'd never want to do it again, couldn't face it, but knew the man holding her close would protect her; she'd learned to trust him that much.

Pushing him away, she patted down his collar and smoothed the lapels of his suit jacket.

'Okay, off you go. Go do what you tycoons do.'

He smiled, ran a fingertip down her cheek before tapping her lightly on the nose. 'See you in two hours.'

'If you talk real fast, maybe one?'

'I'll try.'

As she watched him walk out of the door, utterly gorgeous in a charcoal pinstripe suit, she had to pinch herself to make sure this wasn't all a dream.

They'd landed back in Melbourne and the dream hadn't evaporated. Instead, he'd dropped her at the hotel suite she was staying in until she found a suitable apartment to buy, had raced home to get ready for his meeting and had paid a surprise visit back here on the way.

He must've thought she was a grub because he'd found her the way he'd left her—dishevelled and tired and still wearing the clothes she'd worn on the flight home. All his fault; after he'd dropped her off, she'd mooned about, flicking through travel brochures on India, lolling on the couch, lost in memories, remembering every magical moment of their journey.

The trip had exceeded all her expectations.

She'd discovered a part of her heritage that enthralled her, had finally released the last of her residual anger and had put the past—and Richard—behind her.

And she'd discovered a guy who had been on her periphery until now was in fact the love of her life.

Exceeded? Heck, her expectations had been blasted clean into orbit.

But, for now, she had a date with a shower. She wanted to get cleaned up before heading over to her favourite place in the world: Ambrosia, and right by Ethan's side.

Tamara pocketed her keys, grabbed her bag and was halfway out the door when the phone rang.

She paused, glanced at her watch and decided to let the answering machine pick up in case Ethan had finished early and was waiting for her.

With one ear on the garbled voice coming through the machine, she tapped the side of her head, wondering if water from the shower had clogged her ears. She could've sworn the guy was a reporter from a prominent Melbourne newspaper, the same guy who had hounded her relentlessly after Richard's death. What could he want with her now?

Not interested in anything he had to say, especially on the day she'd landed back in the country, she slammed the door, took the lift to the ground floor, strode through the swank foyer and out into a perfect autumn day.

There was nothing like Melbourne in autumn: the frosty weather, the crisp brown leaves contrasting with the beautiful green in the city parks, the fashionable women striding down Collins Street in high boots and long coats.

She loved it all and as she took a left and headed for Ambrosia, she'd never felt so alive. With a spring in her step, she picked up the pace, eager for her hot chocolate fix—her Ethan fix, more precisely.

Smiling to herself, she passed the newsstand she occasionally bought the odd glossy food magazine from. She may not have worked for a while but she'd kept up with the trends, critically analysing her competitors' work, knowing she could do better if she ever got back to it. That time had come and she couldn't be happier.

However, as she slowed to scan the latest cover of her favourite magazine, her blood froze as her gaze fixed on the headlines advertising today's newspapers.

CELEBRITY CHEF'S MISTRESS HAS LOVE CHILD.

She inhaled a sharp breath, let it out, closed her eyes and opened them.

This was silly. That headline could be referring to any number of celebrity chefs around the world.

With legs suddenly jelly-like, she forced her feet to walk forward, past the newsstand. She'd almost made it when the truth hit her.

The reporter's phone call.

The headline.

No, it couldn't be…

With her lungs screaming for oxygen, she turned back and snatched the nearest newspaper with trembling hands.

'Haven't seen you around here for a while, love?'

She arranged her mouth into a smile for the old guy who'd been working here for ever, when all she wanted to do was flap open the paper and see if the horrible sense of impending doom hanging over her was true.

'Been away.'

She thrust a ten dollar bill at him. 'Here, keep the change.'

'But that's way too much—'

She waved over her shoulder and half ran, half wobbled to the nearest wrought-iron bench, where she collapsed, the newspaper rolled tight in her fist.

It's not about him…it's not about him…

However, no matter how many times she repeated the words, the second she opened the paper and saw Richard's face smiling at her, right next to Sonja's, adjacent to that of an adorable chubby baby with her husband's dimples, the life she'd worked so hard to reassemble crumbled before her very eyes.

She had no idea how she made it to Ambrosia, no recollection of the walk as she unlocked the restaurant and relocked the door before falling onto the nearest chair.

She stared blindly around the room, the place that had become a safe haven for her. The pale lemon walls, the honey oak floorboards, the open fireplace along one wall, the glittering bar along the other—she'd spent every Monday here for the last six months, drinking hot chocolate, honing her work skills, putting her life back together.

A life now laid bare for the public to see and scrutinise and judge.

It had been hard enough discovering Sonja's existence,

the evidence that not only had Richard been cheating on her, but he'd done it in a house bought and paid for by him too while he'd imposed ridiculously tight budgets on her.

She'd been humiliated at the discovery of the other woman, had told no one, and now her degradation would be seen by everyone, her hopes for a new start dashed.

She fisted her hands, pushed them into her eyes in the vain hope to rub away the haunting image of that cherubic baby picture in the newspaper.

That should've been her baby, the baby she'd wanted but Richard had always vetoed, the baby he'd been too busy to have, the baby that would've given her the complete family she always wanted.

She'd pushed for a child, had been placated with lousy excuses and now she'd come face to face with yet more evidence of how much her husband hadn't loved her, how little he'd really thought of her.

Damn him for still having the power to annihilate the self-confidence she'd so carefully rebuilt.

She'd handled his infidelity but this…

Deep sobs racked her body as she bundled the paper into a ball and flung it across the room with an anguished scream.

'What the—' Ethan dropped his briefcase near the back door, where he'd entered, and ran for the main restaurant, where he'd heard the most God-awful sound.

He burst through the swinging doors, his heart leaping to his mouth at the sight that greeted him.

Tam, slumped on a chair, her head buried in her arms while great sobs rent the air, her delicate shoulders heaving.

'Tam?'

He raced across the room, pulled up a chair next to her and reached out to touch her.

'Sweetheart, it's me.'

Her head snapped up and the raw pain radiating from her

red-rimmed eyes slammed into him like a cast-iron skillet. He opened his arms to her, wanting to comfort her, desperate to slay whatever demon had driven her to this.

She shook her head, hiccuped. 'He had a baby.'

Who had a baby?

She wasn't making sense.

With tears coursing down her cheeks, she jerked her thumb towards the floor, where he spied a balled-up newspaper.

He reached it in two strides, smoothing it on the bar, the picture painting a shocking scenario before he sped-read the accompanying article.

Hell, no.

White-hot rage slammed through him, quickly turning to blinding fury as he bunched the newspaper in his fist, searched Tam's face, seeing the truth in every devastated line.

That bastard.

That low-life, lying, cheating, no good, son of a— He sucked in a deep breath.

He needed to support Tam, not fuel his anger. An anger that continued to bubble and stew and threatened to spill over as he watched her swipe her eyes, her hand shaky, her lower lip trembling.

He'd never seen her so bleak, even when she'd lost Rich, the jerk he'd like to personally kill at this very moment if he weren't already dead.

'That baby should've been mine.'

He froze. Surely she didn't mean that?

After what he'd just learned about Rich, about their marriage, how could she have wanted a child by that monster?

'I wanted one, you know.'

She scrambled in her bag for a tissue, her fingers fumbling as she finally found one and used it to great effect. 'More than one. I hated being an only child.'

What could he say? That he thought she was crazy for

wanting kids with Rich? That now, a year after his death, she shouldn't be reacting this way to proof that the guy was scum?

Then it hit him.

What he'd been trying to ignore all along.

She still loved him.

He'd kept his distance all these years, had only made a move now because he'd thought she was over him.

But she wasn't and, despite everything Richard had done, clearly stated in that paper for the world to see, she still wasn't over him.

His hands balled into instant fists, frustration making him want to pound the table.

It was the reason why he hadn't rushed her at the start, this fear that she still had feelings for Richard, the fear that he'd just be the rebound guy, no matter how long he waited.

He'd put it down to his own insecurities, had ignored the twinge of doubt, had taken a chance by letting his iron-clad control slip for the first time ever.

He'd made a monumental mistake, just as he'd feared. Losing control, allowing emotions to rule, only led to one thing: disaster.

'I don't believe this.'

Her red-rimmed eyes sought his, her expression bleak. But she didn't reach out to him and he wanted her to. Damn it, he wanted her to need him, to want him, to love him.

As much as he loved her.

The realisation sent him striding from the table to behind the bar, desperate to put something concrete and solid between them.

He'd made enough of an idiot of himself over her without adding an inopportune declaration to the mix.

She didn't need his love. How could she, when she was still pining for Richard?

She wished her late husband's girlfriend's baby was hers.

He couldn't compete with that. He couldn't compete with the memory of a dead guy. He didn't want to.

'I'm sorry you're going through this.' He switched on the espresso machine, needing to keep busy, needing to obliterate the driving need to vault the bar and bundle her in his arms. 'Coffee? Or a hot chocolate?'

She stilled before his very eyes, her hands steadying as she pushed her chair back, her legs firm as she stood and crossed the restaurant to lean on the bar.

Confusion clouded her eyes. 'I thought you'd be more understanding about this.'

'Oh, I understand a lot more than you think.'

Silently cursing his hasty response, he turned away and busied himself with getting cups ready.

'What's that supposed to mean?'

Rubbing a hand across the back of his neck, he swivelled to face her, trying not to slam the cups onto the bar.

'I've never seen you this upset, even after he died.'

He had time to swallow his words, clamp down on the urge to blurt out exactly what he was thinking. But nothing would be the same after this anyway, so why not tell her the truth? Go for broke?

'Yet here you are, wishing that child was yours.'

He shook his head, poured milk into a stainless-steel jug for frothing to avoid looking at her shattered expression.

'I don't get it. I've just learned the guy I thought I knew had a mistress he shacked up with whenever he could and he had a kid with her, yet here you are, still affected by him. Makes me wonder why.'

When she didn't respond, he glanced up, the emerald fire in her eyes surprising him. She'd gone from quivering victim to furious in a second.

'Why don't you go ahead and tell me what you think? You seem to have done a pretty good job until now.'

He didn't deserve her anger—Rich did, and somehow the fact that she'd turned on him when she should've turned to him lit a fuse to his own smouldering discontent.

'Fine. You want to know what I think?'

His palms slammed onto the bar as he leaned towards her. 'I think Richard left a lasting legacy. I think you're so hung up on the guy you can't get past him, maybe you never will. And I think as long as you let your past affect you this way, you won't have the future you deserve.'

Derision curled her upper lip, her eyes blazing, but not before he'd seen the pain as he scored a direct hit.

'What future is that? With you?'

She made it sound as if she'd rather change that baby's diapers for a lifetime than be with him and he turned away, anguish stabbing him anew.

He had his answer.

She'd just confirmed every doubt he'd ever had—that he'd never live up to King Richard in her heart.

'You know, this place has been a safe haven for me lately. Not any more.'

Her heels clacked against the floorboards as she marched to the table, scooped up her bag and headed for the door.

He watched her in the back mirror, his heart fracturing, splintering, with every step she took.

He could've called out, stopped her, run after her.

Instead, he watched the woman he loved walk out of the door.

CHAPTER THIRTEEN

THE drive down the EastLink Freeway passed in a blur. It was as if she'd been on autopilot ever since she'd stormed out of Ambrosia, hell-bent on putting the past behind her, once and for all.

Ethan was wrong. Dead wrong. About everything.

Except one thing: she had no hope of moving forward unless she confronted her past and that was why she was here in the peaceful ocean retreat of Cape Schanck, clutching a crumpled piece of paper in her hand, staring at the address written in a woman's flowing script, her heart pounding as she slowly looked up at the beautiful beach house.

Richard had been careful to hide his infidelity from her while he'd been alive but she'd found this in an old wallet in the back of his wardrobe after he'd died.

She'd been clearing out his stuff, donating his designer suits to charity and had come across it. At the time, she hadn't cared what it meant but later, when she'd discovered his private appointment diary detailing every sordid detail, along with a stack of emails complete with pictures, it had all made sense.

Cape Schanck. Haven for gold-digging mistresses. And their illegitimate babies.

She blinked several times, determined not to cry. This wasn't a time for tears. She had to do this, had to get on with her life before the bitterness and anger threatened to consume her again; there was no way she'd go back to living the way she had been before India.

Taking a steadying breath, she strode to the front door and knocked twice, loudly.

As she waited, she noticed the spotless cream-rendered walls, the duck egg blue trim, the soft grey shingles. The garden was immaculate, with tulips in vibrant pinks and yellows spilling over the borders, the lawn like a bowling green, and she swallowed the resentment clogging her throat at the thought of Richard tending this garden, on his hands and knees in the dirt, with *her*.

She knocked again, louder this time, feeling foolish. She'd driven the hour and a half down here, fuelled by anger and the driving need to forget, yet hadn't counted on Sonja not being here.

As she was about to turn away, she heard footsteps and braced herself, thrusting her hands into the pockets of her trench coat to stop herself from reaching out and wrapping them around the other woman's neck when she opened the door.

The door swung open and she came face to face with the woman who had stolen her life.

Sonja Van Dyke was stunning, a Dutch supermodel who had graced the catwalks for years in her late teens and, even now, couldn't be more than twenty-five.

She'd taken Australia by storm when she'd first arrived and was rumoured to be making her television debut on a reality show any day now.

Considering how she'd just splashed her sordid affair with Richard all over the tabloids with gay abandon, heaven help her, for who knew what gems she'd drop on live TV?

Even though they'd never met, instant recognition lit the redhead's extraordinary blue eyes as she took a step back, her hand already swinging the door shut.

'Wait.' Tamara stepped forward, wedged her foot in the doorjamb.

With a toss of her waist-length titian hair, Sonja straightened her shoulders as if preparing to do battle. 'I've got nothing to say to you.'

'Well, I've got plenty to say to you.'

Her eyes turned flinty as a smug smile curved the mouth that must've kissed her husband's. The thought should've made her physically ill but now she'd arrived, had seen this woman, all she felt was relief.

She'd done it. Confronted her demons. Now all she had to do was slay them and she could walk away, free.

'It's not a good time for me. Little Richie will be waking from his nap soon.'

Just like that, her relief blew away on the blustery ocean breeze, only to be replaced by the familiar fury that one man had stolen so much from her.

Her dignity, her identity, her pride, and she'd be damned if she stood here and let his mistress steal anything else from her.

'Tough. You need to hear what I have to say.'

She drew on every inner reserve of strength, determined to get this out and walk away head held high.

'By making this fiasco public, you've guaranteed a media frenzy for a month at least. Just keep me out of it. Richard owed me that much at least.'

Sonja drew herself up to an impressive five-eleven and glared down at her. 'Who the hell are you to tell me what I can and can't say? As for Richie owing you, you meant nothing to him.'

She ignored the deliberate provocation of the last statement, needing to get through this and slam the door on her past once and for all.

'I don't give a damn what you say as long as I'm left out of it—'

'Did you know I was six weeks pregnant when Richie died? He was so happy. Thrilled he was going to be a daddy.'

Her blue eyes narrowed, glittering with malice. 'He was going to leave you, you know. Over, just like that.'

She snapped her fingers, her cold smile triumphant.

Tamara's resolution wavered as a fresh wave of pain swamped her. Richard had known about the baby, had continued to come home to her every night and play the dutiful husband while preparing to leave her.

Her belly rolled with nausea and she gulped in fresh air like a fish stranded on a dock, willing the spots dancing before her eyes to fade.

'As for little Richie, he's going to be just as famous as his mama and daddy. That's why I waited until now to sell my story and have him photographed.'

Her eyes gleamed with malice. 'He had terrible jaundice for the first eight weeks and would've looked awful. But now, at four months, he's absolutely gorgeous. Ready for stardom, like his parents.'

Just like that, she realised nothing she could say to this woman would get through to her. She'd been a fool to come here, to try and reason with her.

Being confronted by reports and pictures of Richard and herself in the newspapers and glossy magazines every day for a fortnight when he'd died had driven her mad and now the tabloids would have a field day. This could go on for months; she'd hoped by appealing to Sonja she might refrain from fuelling the story.

But she'd been an idiot. There was no reasoning with the woman. She wanted to relaunch her career and was planning on using her affair with Richard and their child to do it.

She'd never be free of them, free of the scandal, free of the whispers and pitying glances behind her back.

She had to get out of here, escape.

Like a welcome oasis for a thirsty desert traveller, the image of Colva Beach, the Taj Mahal, shimmered into her mind's eye.

There was a place she'd never be plagued by her past, continually reminded of her foolishness in trusting a man totally wrong for her.

A place linked to her heritage, a place filled with hope, a place she could dream and create the future she deserved.

A place she would return to as soon as possible.

'Richie trusted me implicitly. He'd back me one hundred per cent on this, as he always did. Nothing like the love of a good man to give a woman courage to face anything, wouldn't you say?'

Sonja's sickly sweet spite fell on deaf ears—until the implication of what she'd said hit her.

She had a guy who backed her one hundred per cent, who'd travelled all the way to India to do it.

A guy who'd given her courage to start afresh.

A guy who deserved to hear the truth, no matter how humiliating for her.

Walking out on Ethan had been a mistake. A rash, spur-of-the-moment action fuelled by that stupid newspaper article.

She'd been living a lie, had thought she'd put the past behind her, only to have it come crashing down around her and, rather than tell him everything, she'd run.

How ironic—it had taken a cheap tart like Sonja to point out what had been staring her in the face.

Without saying a word, she turned on her heel and headed down the garden path towards the car.

'You're just as spineless as Richie said you were.'

The parting barb bounced off her and she didn't break stride. Nothing Sonja could do or say could affect her now.

Coming here might've been stupid but it had been cathartic. She'd soon be free of her past.

And ready to face her future.

Ethan stepped out of the limo in front of Ambrosia and dropped his travel case at his feet.

He'd thrown himself back into business since Tam had walked out on him four days ago, making flying visits to Sydney, Brisbane and Cairns.

Facilitating meetings, presenting figures, convincing investors, he'd done it all in a nonstop back-to-back whirl of meetings but he was done, drained, running on empty.

Earlier that week he'd landed back in the country, had lost the woman he loved on the same day and buried his head in business as usual to cope; little wonder he could barely summon the energy to step inside.

He stood still for a moment, the slight chill of a brisk autumn evening momentarily clearing his head as he watched patrons pack his restaurant to the rafters.

Intimate tables for two where couples with secretive smiles held hands, tables filled with happy families squabbling over the biggest serving of sticky date pudding, tables where businessmen like himself absentmindedly forked the delicious crispy salt and pepper calamari into their mouths while shuffling papers and making annotations.

He loved this place, had always loved it. It was his baby, his home.

Then why the awful, hollow feeling that some of the gloss had worn off?

He should be punching the air. He'd had a lucky escape. Tam had made her true feelings clear before he was in too deep.

Though what could be deeper than falling in love with a woman he could never have?

With a shake of his head, he picked up his bag and headed

in, the warmth from the open fire on the far side instantly hitting him as the fragrant aromas of garlic, bread fresh from the oven and wok-sizzled beef enveloped him.

He was home and the sooner he banished thoughts of his failed relationship with Tam the better.

'Hey, boss, how was the trip?'

He mustered a tired smile for Fritz, his enthusiastic barman. 'Busy.'

'I bet. Want a drink?'

'A double shot espresso would be great.' He patted his case. 'Help me get through these projections. I'll take it upstairs.'

Fritz saluted. 'No worries.'

As he turned away, Fritz called out, 'Almost forgot. Tamara's popping in soon. She came in earlier, asked when you'd be back and I told her. Said she'd come back.'

His heart bucked and he carefully blanked his expression before nodding. 'Thanks. Give me a buzz when that coffee's ready. And throw in a hot chocolate for her.'

'Shall do, boss.'

He trudged up the stairs to his office, too weary for this confrontation. If it had happened a few days earlier, when he hadn't had time to mull over his foolishness, he might've been more receptive to hearing what she had to say.

But now? What could she say that would change any of this?

She was still in love with her dead husband.

He was in love with her.

A no-win situation, something he never dwelled on in business and he'd be damned if he wasted time wishing things were different now.

After flinging his bag down and bumping the door shut with his hip, he headed to his desk and sank into the chair, rubbing his temples.

They'd both been angry that day she'd walked out. They'd probably had a case of mild jet lag, but that didn't explain her reaction to that baby. Strange thing was, she'd been more upset by the baby than her husband's infidelity.

Unless… He sat bolt upright.

She must've known about the affair.

But for how long? Surely a woman of her calibre wouldn't put up with anything like that?

Something niggled at the edge of his thoughts, something she'd said in India… Another bolt of enlightenment struck as he remembered her saying something about wives putting up with their husbands to keep the peace or some such thing…

The ache behind his temples intensified as the impact of what he was contemplating hit him.

He'd thought he'd known Rich: capable, gregarious, master in the kitchen. But while Rich may have been a talented chef, it looked like he'd had another side to him, a side that made him want to knock his teeth in.

A tentative knock had him striding to the door and yanking it open, all his logical self-talk from the last few days fleeing as he stared at Tam, looking cool and composed in a simple black dress, her eyes wide and wary as they met his.

'I needed to see you.'

Stepping back, he gritted his teeth against the overpowering urge to sweep her into his arms. 'Come in.'

'How've you been?'

He gestured towards the stack of paperwork on his desk. 'Busy. Business as usual.'

She didn't glance at the desk, her wide-eyed gaze fixed on him instead. 'Yeah, Fritz told me you'd been away since the day we got back.'

Shrugging, he indicated she take a seat. 'Duty calls.'

'I admire that about you.'

He searched her face for an indication that she was anything but sincere and came up lacking. But there was something in her tone, as if she was judging him for his work ethic.

'Your ability to slot back into the groove as if nothing has happened.'

'Oh, plenty's happened. I just think I'm better suited to business than figuring out what happened with us.'

She winced and he clenched his hands into fists, thrust them into his pockets to stop from hitting himself in the head for letting that slip out.

His legendary control vanished around this woman, shot down, like his hopes of ever being anything more than a holiday romance for her.

'I overreacted the other day. I'm sorry.'

'Hey, you had every right to overreact.'

He paused, hating to dredge up pain for her but needing to know. 'Did you know Rich was cheating on you?'

Her slow nod had his fists bunching, as he wondered for the hundredth time in the last few days what sort of a jerk would screw around on an amazing woman like Tam.

'I had my suspicions and discovered the truth after he died, but I had no idea about the baby.'

'That must've hurt.'

To his surprise, she shrugged, as if it meant little. 'It did at the time. Made me crazy for a while but I'm over it now. I've moved on.'

She perched on the edge of his desk, so close, so temptingly close. 'Thanks to you.'

'Rebound guy.'

The words were out before he could stop them and she frowned, looking more formidable than he'd ever seen her.

'What?'

'You heard me.'

'You think you're my rebound guy?'

'Yeah.'

Her laughter shocked him as much as her quick swivel towards him, leaving her legs dangling precariously close to him, so close they brushed his arm.

'You're not rebound guy. You're *the* guy.'

He had no idea what she meant, was too confused by her nearness to ask.

Was she deliberately trying to provoke him? Get him to touch her? His palms tingled with the urge to do just that and he kept his hands firmly lodged in his pockets.

'The guy I want to have a future with. The guy who has helped me learn to trust again. The guy I'm in love with.'

His gaze zeroed in on hers, searching for some signal that the stress of the last few days had sent her batty.

All he saw were clear green eyes locked on his, eyes brimming with sincerity and tears and love, the latter enough to catapult him out of the chair and reach for her before he could think twice.

'Say it again.'

She smiled, blinked several times. 'I love you. Can't believe I'm actually saying those words to a guy like you, but there you go.'

He gripped her arms, his initial elation dimming. 'A guy like me?'

'The ultimate playboy, remember? Serial dater? Guy voted most likely to break a woman's heart?'

'Who said that?'

Her lips twitched and he itched to cover them with his. 'Okay, so I made that last bit up. But I have to tell you, loving you is the ultimate risk for me.'

'Because of what Rich did to you?'

To her credit, she didn't flinch or react when he mentioned the jerk's name.

'Because I'd sworn never to trust another guy again.'

She cupped his cheek. 'But you're not just any guy, are you?'

She'd put her heart on the line for him. The least he could do was give her a healthy dose of honesty in return.

'No, I'm the guy who doesn't do emotion. I'm the guy who's a control freak, who's so damned scared of letting go that I almost messed up the best thing to ever happen to me.'

'What's that?'

'You.'

He crushed his mouth to hers, devouring her, hungering for this kiss like a starving man being offered a Michelin-starred buffet.

The kiss went on for ever, a fiery union of two people who couldn't get enough of each other.

How he wished that were true.

In reality, he was chary. For while Tam thought she loved him, he couldn't get the image of her reacting to Rich's baby out of his head; the same head that warned him to tread carefully, as always.

He'd had time to think, time to take back control of his uncharacteristically wavering emotions and, whatever happened, he knew he couldn't simply pick up where they'd left off.

As the kiss gentled, their lips reluctant to disengage, he hugged her, tight.

She'd fallen in love with him and, whether it was on the rebound or not, he knew what it must've cost her to come here and tell him.

'I've got something to tell you.'

He pulled back, searched her face for a clue to the sombre edge in her voice.

'I'm going back to India.'

Fear ricocheted through him, a fear he'd long conquered. Fear that no matter how badly he wanted something, when he could almost taste it, it was snatched out of his reach.

He'd battled the fear when on the streets, when first taken

in by Arnaud, when he'd clawed his way to the top, expecting at every turn to have his goal taken away.

With success, he'd expected to lose the fear but here it was, rearing its ugly head and tormenting him anew.

'For another trip?'

She gnawed at her bottom lip, shook her head. 'I'll never be free of the past as long as I stay here. I want to make a fresh start and I can do that over there.'

The fear coalesced, consolidated, pounding in his ears, yelling that he'd lost her before they'd really started.

'I love you but I have to do this, for me.'

His shocked gaze collided with hers, the depth of her feeling evident in the way she looked at him with stars in her eyes.

She loved him.

She was leaving.

So much for being back in control. His wildly careening emotions swung between exaltation that she returned his love to despair that she'd snatched it out of reach before they'd really begun.

'Ethan? Say something.'

Releasing her, he turned away, needing breathing space, needing time to think.

What could he say?

That he loved her so much it'd kill him to see her walk away now?

That he loved her but couldn't contemplate following her for fear of losing ground with the one solid, reliable thing in his life—his business?

That, until recently, being the number one restaurateur in the world was his dream but, thanks to her, his dream had changed?

He could say any of those things. Instead, he had a sinking feeling that his lifelong need to control everything would eradicate his dream.

He'd fought long and hard to conquer the insecurities borne

from being dumped by a mother who didn't love him, of enduring beatings from older step-siblings, from sleeping in doorways and foraging for scraps of food to fill the ache ravaging his empty belly.

Nothing intimidated him any more. In the business arena, he was king.

Yet right at this moment, with Tam's declaration echoing through his head, haunting him, taunting him, he was catapulted back to a time where he felt sick to his stomach with fear.

Fear he'd lose total control and there'd be no coming back.

Dragging a hand through his hair, he turned back to face her, met her eyes, saw his fear reflected there.

'Not very often I'm lost for words, huh?'

'Try never.'

Her bottom lip wobbled, slugging him to his soul, before she squared her shoulders.

'I'm not asking anything of you.' She waved around the office, pointed at the stack of paperwork on his desk. 'I know you've got a business to run but if you take another holiday, you know where to find me.'

'Where will you be?'

'Agra for the first month or two. I'll probably haunt the Taj for the first fortnight. There was so much more I wanted to see. Then back to Goa. I'll base myself there, start looking for a place to live and exploring job opportunities then.'

His heart almost burst with pride as he saw her standing there, confident in what she wanted, in stark contrast to the fragile woman of a few months ago. She'd come so far.

And she loved him.

It all came back to that. Considering what Rich had done to her, for her to trust him enough with her love let alone be honest about it, blew him away.

With her on another continent, damned if he knew what to do about it.

'You're amazing, you know that?'

He slid his arms around her, hugged her close, wishing he could hold her like this for ever.

'I do now.'

Her voice wavered and he cuddled her tighter, wishing he could throw caution to the wind and follow her to the ends of the earth.

She settled into his embrace for a moment before placing her palms against his chest and pushing away.

'I better go.'

He frowned, tipped her chin up, hating the hint of sadness, resignation, in her voice.

'Don't we have time to—'

'My flight leaves tonight.' She held her hand over his lips, pressed lightly, as if imprinting his lips on her palm. 'I have to go.'

He opened his mouth to respond, to tell her to stay, to give them time, to explore the incredible, wondrous love they'd opened their hearts to.

But he couldn't do that to her, couldn't put his needs in front of hers. He'd be damned if he treated her in any way remotely like that bastard Richard.

This was *her* time.

He loved her enough to let her go.

'My Tam.'

He caressed her cheek, his fingertips skating across her skin, imprinting the feel of her into his memory to dredge up at the end of a long day.

Tipping her chin up, his gaze skimmed her face, memorising every detail and, when his gaze collided with hers, the pain in her shimmering eyes took his breath away.

'I'll miss you.'

Before he could move she plastered her lips to his, a swift, impassioned kiss filled with the yearning clamouring at his soul, breaking the kiss when he tried to hold on to her.

'Tam!'

'Maybe I'll see you at the Taj some time.'

With wooden legs rooted to the spot, he watched her hurried yet dignified exit, stifling the urge to chase and beg her to stay, the dull ache in his chest spreading, gutting him.

He rubbed at his chest, pacing his office like one of the tigers they'd seen at a National Park.

The ache gnawed at him, eating away a large hole that soon flooded with a sickening mix of regret and frustration and fear. Fear that he'd lost her—for good.

Maybe with distance, time apart, he could figure out what to do. The thought alone made a mockery of his need for time.

Time for what? Time to second-guess himself at every turn? Time to dredge up every reason why he couldn't do this? Time to dissociate from the crazy, wild, out-of-control feeling loving Tam fostered?

The way he saw it, he was all out of time.

She'd had the guts to lay it all on the line for him. So what was he going to do about it?

Real life was far from rosy and happy endings usually required a hell of a lot of hard work and compromise. He knew that better than anyone else.

But he wanted that happy ending, craved it with every ravenous cell in his body.

His gaze lighted on the phone. He had the resources and the contacts worldwide to make anything happen.

How hard could it be to organise his life for the next month or so in order to follow the woman he loved?

Snatching up the phone, he punched in numbers.

Only one way to find out.

CHAPTER FOURTEEN

TAMARA lay back on the wooden massage table, wriggling around to get comfortable while latching onto the skimpy towel in an effort to cover her breasts.

Her mum had extolled the virtues of Ayurvedic therapies at length, a firm believer that all aspects of life, from people to animals to diseases, were combinations of the three energy elements: air, fire and water.

Apparently, her *dosha*—constitution—was predominantly air, which explained why she was prone to worry, anxiety and the occasional bout of nerves.

Right now, she was all three as the therapist, a woman of indeterminate age dressed in a simple white sari, positioned a pot of hot oil directly over her head.

'Relax. This will help rebalance you.'

Easy for her to say. She wasn't the one about to get hot oil dripped onto her forehead.

However, as the first trickle flowed gently onto her forehead, she exhaled in relief and closed her eyes, filled with a serenity she'd been craving for a week.

Coming back to India was supposed to centre her, help her feel safe, and while she'd been more grounded in the last seven days than she had in a while, a strange restlessness still gripped her.

She'd expected an instant fix coming back here. Crazy, considering what she'd been through, but at least she could relax here without fear of opening a newspaper or turning on a television to find evidence of Richard's disregard leering at her.

The oil stream stopped as she squinted through one eye, watching the woman straightening the oil pot before she delved bony fingers through her hair to her scalp.

'Too tense, too tense.' She tut-tutted, digging her fingers deeper until Tamara sighed, determined to ignore her negative thoughts and luxuriate under the expert tutelage of massaging fingers.

'Breathe. Let the oils help you.'

Great, she'd stumbled across another wannabe fortune-teller.

Though, from the tension in her muscles, it didn't take a psychic to figure out she was anxious about something.

'Sandalwood is good for stress, frankincense for fear, gardenia for anger. Breathe, let the oils work for you.'

Yeah, she was stressed. Discovering your husband was a lying, cheating hound and his mistress had just told the world about it led to loads of stress. Not to mention the baby bonus.

And she was scared—scared she'd made the wrong decision in leaving behind the one man who'd brought joy to her life in a very long time.

As for anger, she'd thought she'd left all that behind when she'd walked away from Sonja and all she stood for.

'Your *dosha* needs soothing, many treatments. Abhyanga and aromatherapy today, meditation tomorrow, colour and gem therapy the day after. Yes?'

She could handle abhyanga—this massage really was to die for—and the oils and meditation at a pinch, but she had the feeling that this wise woman was giving her a sales pitch along with the amateur psychobabble.

Mumbling a noncommittal response, she concentrated on relaxing her muscles, blanking her mind.

It didn't work.

Her thoughts zoomed straight back to Ethan.

What was he thinking? Doing? Feeling?

It had taken all her limited supply of courage to see him again after she'd stormed out of Ambrosia the day she'd discovered Richard had a love child by his mistress.

But she'd had to—had to tell him the truth. She loved him, trusted him and, while he hadn't said the words back, she now knew he was a man of action rather than words.

His admission, ripped from somewhere deep within, spoke volumes. He was a control freak and, for someone like him, this powerful yet nebulous emotion gripping her would be terrifying.

She understood. But it didn't make the ache gripping her heart any easier, or eradicate the fruitless wish that he could've come with her. She hadn't expected him to, would've argued if he'd suggested it, but that didn't stop the constant yearning she had.

'No good, no good.'

The woman pummelled her thigh muscles, lifted a leg and dropped it. 'Too tense. You go, come back tomorrow.'

She opened her eyes, sat up, clutching the towel to her chest. 'But I paid for an hour.'

The woman waved her away. 'I will give you two hours tomorrow but today—useless. Your muscles—' she banged the wooden table with a fist '—hard as this. Abhyanga not work for you today.'

She opened her mouth to protest again but the woman floated out of the room on a whirl of sari, leaving her cold and semi-naked and ruing her decision to have a massage to unwind.

Maybe she would come back tomorrow.

Then again, she had a feeling that nothing could help release the pent-up tension twisting her muscles into ropes of steel.

Nothing, apart from having Ethan arrive on her doorstep. And that just wasn't going to happen.

He'd been here since daybreak every day for a week, watching the pale dawn bathe the marble monument in translucent light, staying until dusk when the purple streaks turned the Taj luminescent, grateful the law only allowed electric vehicles within ten kilometres of this stunning monument to avoid pollution staining it.

He'd traversed the place from end to end, lingering around the main gateway, oblivious to the beauty of the entwined red lotus flowers, leaves and vines motifs inlaid in semi-precious stones around the niche, always on the lookout.

He'd drifted past the red sandstone mosque on the western side of the Taj and the Taj Mahal Naggar Khana—Rest House—to the east, buoyed by hope.

He'd sat by the tranquil River Yamuna snacking on tiffin packed by the hotel, he'd strolled through the gardens, scanning the crowds for a glimpse of Tam.

Nothing.

An endless week where he'd scoured the Taj Mahal, a shadow to its greatness, drifting to every corner of the magnificent monument with the hope in his heart lending speed to his feet.

He'd walked. And walked. And walked.

Always on the lookout, his gaze darting every which way, following the hordes, desperate for a glimpse of long black hair and sparkling green eyes.

Still nothing.

While the flight details he'd obtained said she'd landed in Delhi, then hopped a train to Agra and hadn't left again, Tam could be anywhere.

Maybe she'd changed her mind about haunting this place, had taken a train, a bus, to goodness knows where. Or she could be holed up in some ashram seeking higher guidance. Or planning a trek up Everest. Or back in Goa already.

Wherever she was, she wasn't here.

He rubbed his eyes, refocused on the crowd heading towards the Taj. This was crazy. A waste of time.

He could spend a lifetime here and she still wouldn't turn up.

This was the last hour.

Come tomorrow, he'd instigate phase two of his plan to track her down. In the meantime, he had one more lap of the grounds to complete.

Tamara's breath caught at her first glimpse of the Taj Mahal, as it did every day she'd come here.

As the sun set the faintest pink blush stole across the marble, the highest dome a breathtaking silhouette against the dusk sky.

Despite the tourists milling around, snapping away, an instant sense of peace infused her and she headed for the back where the river flowed quietly on a familiar path as old as time.

That had been their favourite spot—hers and Ethan's—and, while it may seem foolish, she knew she'd feel closer to him there.

Rounding the corner, she was almost mown down by a pair of rambunctious six-year-olds and, once they'd disentangled themselves, she brushed off her dusty trousers and set off for the river.

A lone figure stood on the banks. A man, dressed in khaki chinos and a white T-shirt. A man whose breadth of shoulders she'd recognise anywhere, whose casual stance, with hands thrust into pockets, heartrendingly familiar and, as the figure sensed her presence, turned, her belly clenched and tumbled with the overwhelming rush of recognition.

A surge of adrenaline urged her to run towards him but

she'd done that before and he, despite her declaration, still hadn't said he loved her.

He could be here for any number of reasons: scoping out another restaurant site, poaching another master chef, a business meeting.

However, as he strode towards her, long, hungry strides rapidly closing the distance between them, she knew he was here for none of those reasons.

The expression on his face told her why he'd come.

And the realisation took her breath away.

CHAPTER FIFTEEN

THEY stopped less than a foot apart, enveloped in uncharacteristic awkwardness.

Tamara didn't know whether to hug him or strangle him—for making her love him, crave him, unable to forget him.

'What are you doing here?'

Ethan smiled, his casual shrug pulling his cotton T-shirt across his shoulders in delicious detail. 'Haunting this place in the hope of finding you.'

He'd come for her and her spirit soared.

'Exactly how long have you been here?'

'About a week.'

'You've been here every day for a week? Are you nuts?'

'Yeah.' He stepped closer, swamping her in warmth and charisma and magic. 'About you.'

Her heart swelled, filled to overflowing with love for this man. But it wasn't that easy. Nothing ever was and she couldn't get carried away because he'd arrived on her doorstep.

He was here but did he love her?

She needed to hear him say it, craved the words more than her next chai fix.

Trying to hide the cobra's nest of nerves twisting and coiling in her belly, she took a step forward, slid her hand into his.

'The feeling's mutual.' She squeezed his hand, knowing his

presence here spoke louder than words ever could but needing to have everything out in the open for them to really move forward. 'Do you know why I chose here to start my new life?'

His fingertips skated over her cheek, lingered on her jaw, before dropping to her shoulder, his touch firm and comforting, as always.

'Because, when we were here, you said it made you feel safe. I get that now, your need for security.'

'Do you? Do you really?' Her gaze searched his, needing reassurance, desperate for it. She wanted to believe him, wanted to believe in him. 'Because I really needed to feel safe when I discovered the baby and you weren't there for me.'

Shadows drifted across his eyes, turning them from startling blue to murky midnight. 'I'm sorry.'

She accepted his apology but it didn't cut it. Not now, after they'd shared so much, been through so much together.

'Why did you shut me out?'

He squeezed her shoulder before releasing it, turning away and dragging a hand through his hair, but not before she'd seen something shocking on his face.

Shame.

Ethan Brooks, the man who had it all, was ashamed.

He dragged in a deep breath, another, before turning back to face her.

'I didn't want to have to tell you this—any of it.'

He was struggling, she could see it in the muscle twitching in his jaw, in his thinly compressed lips. Looked as if she wasn't the only one with enough baggage to bring India's railway system to a screeching halt.

'Tell me. If nothing else, we're still friends.'

His head reared up. 'I want to be more than friends, damn it. I want—'

'Then give us a chance.' She softened her tone, touched his cheek. 'Tell me.'

He raked his hand through his hair again, looking decidedly ruffled and adorable. 'I've never told anyone this.'

She waited, wondering what could rattle him this badly.

'I was jealous that day at Ambrosia, furious you were still hung up over Rich—'

'But I'm not—'

'If you are or aren't doesn't really excuse how I treated you. What really pushed my buttons was not being in control of the situation. And that's something I don't like, not being in control.'

'You've told me. You're a businessman, a successful one, it figures.'

He shook his head. 'That's not the reason.'

He paused and she knew by the bleakness in his eyes that he was leading up to something big.

'I used to be a street kid. Dumped by my mum when I was five, shoved from foster family to family, scrounged on the streets from the age of thirteen.'

Sorrow gripped her heart. 'I had no idea, I'm so sorry.'

A wry smile twisted his mouth. 'We're doing a lot of that—apologising. Not real romantic, is it?'

'This is about honesty.'

As for romance, it would come. Having him open up to her, knowing how much it cost him, told her they had a future—a great one.

'And us.' He scanned her face, searching for reassurance. 'This has always been about us, Tam. I'm not telling you all this for any other reason than to give us a second chance.'

He cupped her chin, tipped it up. 'Do you believe in second chances?'

'You have to ask me that?'

Heck, she was the queen of second chances. She'd given Richard enough of them: after he'd stood her up the first time, after he'd blown her off for a restaurant opening, after she'd caught him groping a waitress within six months of their marriage.

Yet here was this incredibly honest man standing in front of her, his feelings shining bright in his eyes, asking her for a second chance? How loud could she scream yes without getting arrested?

Holding out her hand to him, she said, 'Come on, let's take a walk.'

'That's not exactly the answer I was hoping for.'

She smiled, recognising the instant he glimpsed the love in her eyes—for his eyes widened, all that dazzling blue focused on her.

'I have so much I want to say to you but let's go somewhere quieter.'

He glanced around, puzzlement creasing his brow. 'You can't get much quieter than this. The closest couple is twenty metres away.'

She tapped the side of her nose. 'Trust me, I know somewhere quieter.'

Sliding his hand into hers, she sighed as his fingers intertwined with hers. This felt right, had always felt right from the first moment he'd held her hand at Colva Beach.

Leading him to the furthest corner of the garden, she pointed to a young cypress tree.

'I've come here a few times over the last week. Seems I do my best thinking here.'

His eyebrows shot up. 'You've been here for a week too?'

'I told you I would be. I just didn't expect in my wildest dreams you'd be here too.'

He brushed the barest of kisses across her lips, her eyes welling at his tenderness, but she had to say this, had to make sure he knew where she was coming from.

She slipped her hand out of his, sank down and patted the ground next to her. 'I also came here to think, to figure out some stuff. Seems like every second person in this country is intent on predicting my fortune. I can't even get a massage these days without the therapist giving me a free glimpse into the future.'

He chuckled, sat next to her. 'So what's in the cards?'

She opened her mouth to respond and he held up both hands and waved them in front of her. 'On second thoughts, I don't want to know if they predicted some tall, dark and handsome stranger sweeping you off your feet.'

He winked, his rakish smile so heartrendingly familiar she leaned towards him without realising. 'Unless they mentioned me by name, that is.'

Hugging her knees close, she rested her chin on them, staring at the Taj Mahal, a translucent ivory in the dusk.

'Honestly? I've done so much thinking this last week, I think I can predict my own future pretty accurately.'

She'd sat in this very spot for hours on end, analysing her life, pondering the choices she'd made, knowing she should learn from mistakes of the past in building a better, brighter future.

While she felt safe here, she hadn't quite achieved the peace she'd hoped for, gripped by a relentless restlessness, no matter how many hours she tried meditating.

She knew why.

The reason was staring her in the face with concern in his blue eyes.

'So go ahead. Give it to me straight. What does the future hold for Tamara Rayne?'

Now that the moment of truth had arrived, she balked.

He'd surprised her, turning up when she'd been contemplating some vague, pie-in-the-sky dream, a nebulous idea she'd pondered at great length, debating the logistics of a long-distance relationship, wondering if they could really make it work.

But she couldn't shake off the fear that still dogged her, the fear she'd finally recognised as undermining her relationship with Ethan right from the very beginning.

She shrugged, hugged her knees tighter. 'My future is here. I've put feelers out and loads of the big newspapers are after food critics. Plus I can freelance for some of the glossy magazines and—'

'While it's great your career is back on track, I'm more interested in you. What does the future hold for you?'

Us, was what he really meant.

The unsaid word hovered between them, temptingly within reach if she had the guts to reach out there and grab it.

She took a deep breath and shuffled her bottom around to face him. In the fading light, with the low-hanging branches casting shadows over his face, she couldn't read his expression. And she wanted to, needed to.

He'd come but there'd been no declaration, no emotional reunion, just two people dancing around each other, throwing out the odd bit of truthful information.

Should she put her heart on the line, once and for all? Confront her fear, at the risk of losing the love of her life?

'I guess some of my future depends on you.'

He didn't move a muscle, not the slightest flicker.

'I've done a lot of soul-searching this last week and the only thing I regret in leaving Melbourne is not being completely honest with you.'

'I'm listening.'

She released her arms, shook them out, stretched out her legs, which were cramping as badly as her belly.

'When I ran out of Ambrosia that day, I didn't correct your wrong assumptions. I was too disappointed, too caught up in the moment. I wasn't thinking straight. It wasn't until later, much later, I realised how it must've looked.'

'You still love Richard, I know—'

Her gaze snapped to his, beseeching him to understand.

'No, you don't. I don't love him, I probably never really loved him.'

She bit her bottom lip, knowing she'd sound callous but needing to get this out of her system.

'I'd barely dated before I met him, then suddenly this brash, famous guy is all over me. I was flattered, just a little bit in love and the next thing I know we're married.'

'I always thought you were happy.'

She nodded, slowly. 'We were, for the first few months. I loved being married, loved how safe I felt having a husband who adored me. But then his lies started. And the rest.'

Her heart twisted at the memories of what she'd endured, all in the name of 'for better or worse'.

'He made my life hell. If I wore black, he said I looked too thin. If I wore white, too fat. He belittled my job, saying no one ever read the crap I wrote. He rifled through my handbag and diary to keep tabs on me. He hated what I cooked, threw a chicken Kiev at the wall once.'

'Hell, Tam—'

'He called me a useless bitch too many times to count, used subtle put-downs in front of his friends, demeaned the way I decorated our place, rubbished my friends, disparaged my mum.'

He swore, shook his head but she had to continue now she'd started, had to get this out of her system once and for all.

'Did you know he was a classic passive-aggressive? I started walking around on eggshells, doing the right things, saying the right things, in an effort to avoid the inevitable explosion if things didn't go his way.'

Ethan reached out to her, placed his hand over hers lying on the grass. 'I had no idea.'

'No one did.'

She blinked back tears, swallowed the bitterness. 'How could you, when Richard Downey, Australia's favourite celebrity chef, was all smiles, the life of every party?'

He squeezed her hand. 'Why did you stay?'

She'd asked herself the same question a million times, had come up with different answers.

How could she verbalise her craving for love, for security, for the perfect happily-ever-after scenario her parents had until her dad died?

It sounded so soppy, so stupid, especially after she'd realised Richard could never be that man for her.

'I stayed because I wanted the family I never had after my dad died. I craved it, which is probably half the reason I married him in the first place. As misguided as it sounds, at the time I thought if I could be a good wife, our marriage would stand a fighting chance.'

She wriggled her hand out from under his on the pretext of retwisting her hair into a loose chignon, his touch too painful, too poignant with what she had to say next.

'I became invisible. I lost my identity, my dignity and my self-respect for a man who didn't care about me, no matter what I did. I got caught up in a vicious cycle, trying to convince him I wasn't worthless in order to regain some semblance of self-respect in order to leave him. Round and round I went, trying my guts out, never being good enough, totally helpless. And I'll never forgive myself for that.'

He swore under his breath, bundled her into his arms and she slowly relaxed as he stroked her back in long, comforting caresses. 'It's finished. Over. You're not that person any more.'

But she was the same person, with the same fears dogging her.

Drawing back, he cradled her face in his hands. 'Tam, it's going to be okay.'

'Is it?'

In response, he lowered his head and kissed her, a slow, tender kiss on her lips, a kiss of affirmation and optimism and faith, a kiss filled with promise and hope.

The hope was the clincher.

She had to tell him—all of it.

Reaching up, she trailed her fingertips down his cheek, the familiar rasp of stubble sending a shiver up her arm.

'I know you care about me and you're nothing like Richard. But I've finally found myself again, I'm finally comfortable in my own skin and I don't want to risk losing that. For anyone.'

Wariness crept across his face. 'What are you trying to say?'

'I'm scared to get involved in a relationship again.'

She dropped her hand, wriggled back to put some distance between them. 'I'm willing to date but I can't make any promises.'

'You're wrong.'

Confused, she stared at him.

'I don't just care about you. I love you.'

Her sharp indrawn gasp sounded harsh in the silence and his hand shot out and latched onto her wrist as if he expected her to bolt.

'And I get it. You're scared. Scared to take a chance on a relationship for fear of losing your identity again. But hell, Tam, this is me. Not Richard. Surely you know I'd never hurt you?'

Hot, scalding tears burned the back of her eyes—tears of hope, tears of fear.

If loving Richard and losing herself had been painful, loving Ethan and losing him would be a hundred times worse.

But the fear was still there, still undermining her new-found confidence, whispering insidious warnings that her inner strength could vanish in a second if she made the wrong decision again.

'I know. You just being here is proof enough but I guess the fear has been a part of me so long, it's hard to shake.'

He shook his head, his grip unrelenting. 'Do you think this is easy for me? I've never loved anyone, let alone admitted it. I don't trust easily—'

'Which is why you date those airheads,' she finished for him, the realisation flooring her.

After what he'd told her today—being abandoned by his mum, dumped from family to family—everything suddenly slid into place.

He was just as frightened as her: frightened to love, frightened to get emotionally involved, frightened to lose control.

Yet he'd confronted his fear, overcome it, for her.

'You're as scared as me,' she said in a hushed tone, scrabbling on her knees to get closer to him.

'That's it, isn't it? Why you closed off that day at Ambrosia? You thought I still cared about Richard, about having his baby and you loved me then. You were just hiding your fear, weren't you?'

His slow, reluctant nod had her launching onto his lap and wrapping her arms around his neck. 'Jeez, we're a fine pair. We can read each other's minds, we just don't want to delve into our own.'

He nuzzled her neck, sending a delightful shiver skating across her skin. 'So I take it this means you want to take a risk on an old scaredy-cat like me?'

Laughing, she pulled back, planted a loud, resounding kiss on his mouth.

'You bet.'

She kissed him again—slower this time, much slower—and they came up dragging in great lungfuls of air several long moments later.

'I love you too. The for ever kind of love.'

He smiled, his arms locked firmly around her waist, every ounce of devotion and adoration and love blazing from his guileless blue eyes.

'Is that your prediction?'

'Oh, yeah.'

He jerked his head towards the Taj Mahal, the majestic

monument standing tall and strong, a silent observer of yet another romantic drama playing out in its honour.

'You know, they say this place is mystical. The ultimate dedication to love. So what do you say we live up to its romantic promise?'

She held her breath, her heart racing with anticipation as her mind took a flying leap into the future.

Maybe her predictive powers were developing, for she had a sneaking suspicion Ethan was about to—

'Tam, will you marry me? I promise to love you, cherish you, let you be your own person and do whatever you want.'

His wide smile had her grinning right back at him with elation filling her soul and joy expanding her heart.

'How can a girl refuse a proposal like that?'

'You can't.'

He stole a kiss and she poured all her love for him into it.

'You once asked me if I believed in love at first sight.'

His eyes crinkled adorably, the roguish pirate smile back in place. 'And do you?'

'Whether first sight, short sight or long sight, I believe in loving you.'

As their lips met, the moon rose, casting an enchanting glow over the Taj Mahal and its latest pair of lovers bound by destiny.

**We'll be spotlighting a different series
every month throughout 2009
to celebrate our 60th anniversary.**

Look for Silhouette® Nocturne™ in October!

Travel through time to experience tales
that reach the boundaries of life and death.
Bestselling authors Lindsay McKenna, Cindy
Dees, P.C. Cast and Merline Lovelace join
together in a brand-new, four-book
Time Raiders miniseries.

TIME RAIDERS

August—*The Seeker*
by *USA TODAY* bestselling author Lindsay McKenna

September—*The Slayer* by Cindy Dees

October—*The Avenger*
by *New York Times* bestselling author and
coauthor of the House of Night novels P.C. Cast

November—*The Protector*
by *USA TODAY* bestselling author Merline Lovelace

Available wherever books are sold.

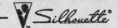

SPECIAL EDITION

FROM *NEW YORK TIMES*
BESTSELLING AUTHOR

SUSAN MALLERY

DESERT
ROGUES

THE SHEIK AND THE BOUGHT BRIDE

Victoria McCallan works in Prince Kateb's palace.
When Victoria's gambling father is caught cheating
at cards with the prince, Victoria saves her father from
going to jail by being Kateb's mistress for six months.
But the darkly handsome desert sheik isn't as harsh as
Victoria thinks he is, and Kateb finds himself attracted to
his new mistress. But Kateb has already loved and lost
once—is he willing to give love another try?

Available in October wherever books are sold.

#1 *New York Times*
bestselling author

DEBBIE MACOMBER

Dear Reader,

I'm not much of a letter writer. As the sheriff here, I'm used to writing incident reports, not chatty letters. But my daughter, Megan—who'll be making me a grandfather soon—told me I had to do this. So here goes.

I'll tell you straight out that I'd hoped to marry Faith Beckwith (my onetime high school girlfriend) but she ended the relationship last month, even though we're both widowed and available.

However, I've got plenty to keep me occupied, like the unidentified remains found in a cave outside town. And the fact that my friend Judge Olivia Griffin is fighting cancer. And the break-ins at 204 Rosewood Lane—the house Faith happens to be renting from Grace Harding…

If you want to hear more, come on over to my place or to the sheriff's office (if you can stand the stale coffee!).

Troy Davis

92 Pacific Boulevard

*Available August 25
wherever books are sold!*

MIRA®

MDM2669

You're invited to join our Tell Harlequin Reader Panel!

By joining our new reader panel you will:

- Receive Harlequin® books—they are FREE and yours to keep with no obligation to purchase anything!
- Participate in fun online surveys
- Exchange opinions and ideas with women just like you
- Have a say in our new book ideas and help us publish the best in women's fiction

In addition, you will have a chance to win great prizes and receive special gifts! See Web site for details. Some conditions apply. Space is limited.

To join, visit us at
www.TellHarlequin.com.

REQUEST YOUR FREE BOOKS!
2 FREE NOVELS PLUS 2
FREE GIFTS!

HARLEQUIN®

Romance.

From the Heart, For the Heart

YES! Please send me 2 FREE Harlequin® Romance novels and my 2 FREE gifts (gifts are worth about $10). After receiving them, if I don't wish to receive any more books, I can return the shipping statement marked "cancel". If I don't cancel, I will receive 4 brand-new novels every month and be billed just $3.84 per book in the U.S. or $4.24 per book in Canada. That's a savings of at least 15% off the cover price! It's quite a bargain! Shipping and handling is just 50¢ per book.* I understand that accepting the 2 free books and gifts places me under no obligation to buy anything. I can always return a shipment and cancel at any time. Even if I never buy another book, the two free books and gifts are mine to keep forever.

114 HDN EYU3 314 HDN EYKG

Name	(PLEASE PRINT)	

Address		Apt. #

City	State/Prov.	Zip/Postal Code

Signature (if under 18, a parent or guardian must sign)

Mail to the Harlequin Reader Service:
IN U.S.A.: P.O. Box 1867, Buffalo, NY 14240-1867
IN CANADA: P.O. Box 609, Fort Erie, Ontario L2A 5X3

Not valid to current subscribers of Harlequin Romance books.

**Are you a subscriber of Harlequin Romance books
and want to receive the larger-print edition?
Call 1-800-873-8635 today!**

* Terms and prices subject to change without notice. Prices do not include applicable taxes. Sales tax applicable in N.Y. Canadian residents will be charged applicable provincial taxes and GST. Offer not valid in Quebec. This offer is limited to one order per household. All orders subject to approval. Credit or debit balances in a customer's account(s) may be offset by any other outstanding balance owed by or to the customer. Please allow 4 to 6 weeks for delivery. Offer available while quantities last.

Your Privacy: Harlequin Books is committed to protecting your privacy. Our Privacy Policy is available online at www.eHarlequin.com or upon request from the Reader Service. From time to time we make our lists of customers available to reputable third parties who may have a product or service of interest to you. If you would prefer we not share your name and address, please check here. ☐

HR09R

Coming Next Month

Available October 13, 2009

Look for the second books in both Marion Lennox's royal trilogy and Barbara Hannay's baby duet, plus makeovers, miracles and marriage, come to Harlequin® Romance!

#4123 THE FRENCHMAN'S PLAIN-JANE PROJECT Myrna Mackenzie
In Her Shoes...
Bookish and shy, Meg longs to be poised and confident. There's more than a simple makeover in store when she's hired by seductive Frenchman Etienne!

#4124 BETROTHED: TO THE PEOPLE'S PRINCE Marion Lennox
The *Marrying His Majesty* miniseries continues.
Nikos is the people's prince, but the crown belongs to the reluctant Princess Athena, whom he was forbidden to marry. He must convince her to come home....

#4125 THE GREEK'S LONG-LOST SON Rebecca Winters
Escape Around the World
Self-made millionaire Theo can have anything his heart desires. But there's just one thing he wants—his first love, Stella, and their long-lost son.

#4126 THE BRIDESMAID'S BABY Barbara Hannay
Baby Steps to Marriage...
In the conclusion to this miniseries, unresolved feelings resurface as old friends Will and Lucy are thrown together as best man and bridesmaid. But a baby is the last thing they expect.

#4127 A PRINCESS FOR CHRISTMAS Shirley Jump
Christmas Treats
Secret princess Mariabella won't let anyone spoil her seaside haven. So when hotshot property developer Jake arrives, she'll stand up to all gorgeous six feet of him!

#4128 HIS HOUSEKEEPER BRIDE Melissa James
Heart to Heart
Falling for the boss wasn't part of Sylvie's job description. But Mark's sad eyes intrigue her and his smile makes her melt. Before she knows it, this unassuming housekeeper's in over her head!